THE CASE OF THE
MISSING LIGHTNING BAT

AN EVAN SINCLAIR MYSTERY

Happy Reading,

VICTOR D. EVANS

Loch Ness Books

Loch Ness Books

MECHANICSBURG, PENNSYLVANIA

an imprint of Sunbury Press, Inc.
Mechanicsburg, PA USA

NOTE: This is a work of fiction. Names, characters, places and incidents are the product of the author's imagination or are used fictitiously, and any resemblance to actual persons, living or dead, business establishments, events or locales is entirely coincidental.

For information about special discounts for bulk purchases, please contact Sunbury Press Orders Dept. at (855) 338-8359 or orders@sunburypress.com.

To request one of our authors for speaking engagements or book signings, please contact Sunbury Press Publicity Dept. at publicity@sunburypress.com.

ISBN: 978-1-62006-902-8 (Trade paperback)

FIRST LOCH NESS BOOKS EDITION: November 2021

Product of the United States of America
0 1 1 2 3 5 8 13 21 34 55

Set in Garamond
Designed by Chris Fenwick
Cover by Melinda Burt
Edited by Chris Fenwick

Continue the Enlightenment!

For Mother, my biggest fan, and

LGBTQ youth everywhere:

We see you; we love you…

CHAPTER 1

THE POWER HITTER

"Today is the day," I said under my breath. Sixth grade had been rough, really rough. This year the universe owed me.

A sudden surge of energy shot throughout my entire body. I pushed my chair back from the table — releasing a heavy breath — closed my eyes, and turned up the volume on my earbuds, which blasted Rascal Flatt's 'These Days' on my favorite country music channel. "It's now or never."

I knew Mom, my guardian angel, was looking down on me, and then there was my dad, who would just say, "Man up, Evan!"

I took a deep breath, brushed the breadcrumbs from my green polo, and removed my earbuds. I planted my feet firmly on the floor to stand when I heard a voice behind me.

"Give it back, Christian! I know you have it."

I looked over my shoulder to see everyone fixated on Jayden Stevens, a 5'8" porcelain-skinned beanpole planted in the middle of the lunchroom, his fists clenched down by his side. His stringy brown hair lopped over his forehead as he squinted so tightly you could barely see his hazel eyes.

Being African-American and only 5'5" with medium-brown skin and close-cut black curly hair, I was Jayden's polar opposite.

"I don't need your stupid *Thor* bat. I have real talent." Christian Carlson stood across from Jayden, running his fingers through his auburn hair. He was at least a half-foot shorter than Jayden, but his small stature never thwarted his unscrupulous behavior.

"Yeah, right." Jayden moved closer to Christian. "Give it back now, or you're going to get a serious beatdown."

Christian's response was to take another step forward, rise to his tippy toes and stare into the most popular guy in the school's eye before he said, "Bring it."

A couple of the *bros* - aka my daily tormentors - moved to stand behind Christian, their leader. Some of the *untouchables* - aka the popular kids – assembled behind Jayden. Oh no, things were going to pop off. So much for my plan to attempt to sit at the untouchables' table. Today wasn't the day after all.

I nervously picked up my sandwich to make a quick getaway when someone bumped my chair, causing a gob of mayonnaise to land on my shirt.

"Get out of the way, Sissy Sinclair," one of the bros yelled. My face burned as I scooted my chair forward, squeezing myself closer to the edge of the table until I could hardly breathe.

I turned around, but all I could see were random bodies being pushed and pulled in different directions. Jayden must have taken Christian at his word, and he brought it, resulting in a free-for-all.

I smirked, thinking how Dad constantly ragged on me for using too much mayo when I made my lunch. I reached for a napkin and began to wipe the goo off my shirt when my chair was rammed again, causing the mayo to smear up the shirt, almost to my neck.

The Lincoln Middle School cafeteria was a war zone. It was like a teenage episode of *Star Trek* where every faction had their designated sections, and like Klingons and Ferengi, certain groups should not intermix. That included the bros and untouchables.

"Break it up . . . *Now.*" Mrs. McCormack raised her voice over the chaos. "Unless you all want to take a trip to the principal's office." She must have been the lucky teacher on lunchroom duty today.

The ache in my chest sharpened, although I couldn't tell if it was from being pressed up against the table or my perpetual discontent. Today was supposed to change all of that.

I momentarily forgot about the pain when I looked over and saw Kyle Reynolds, the jock of all jocks, dressed in a red pullover, perfectly complementing his bright blue eyes as he followed Jayden back to the untouchable's table. I didn't want to admit it but seeing him always made my pulse race.

That's why this was my favorite spot in the caf. It gave me the perfect vantage point of the untouchables. I looked over to see them returning to their seats, laughing and frolicking. Obviously, they thought they'd won that altercation. As they sat down, it was like they were on their own blissful cloud surrounded by a circle of heavenly light. If they were on cloud nine, I wasn't even near cloud one.

I could still go over there. I looked down at my mayo-stained shirt and sighed; all the mojo I'd mustered spurted from my pores like a sprinkler. It was all ruined. My first attempt to sit with the untouchables had to be perfect. *Maybe I'll try again tomorrow.*

"Did you have to go accuse him like that?" Kyle spat while running his fingers through his short spiky blond hair. "You're lucky I had your back."

"I could have handled him," Jayden rebuffed.

Kyle twisted his lower lip. "All five of them, Jay-Thor? I'm sick of all your moaning about Thor. You haven't stopped talking about it since you lost that bat last weekend."

Another reason I loved this spot – I could hear everything they said. I turned to sneak another peek at Kyle. He was on the shorter side—only about five feet, three inches tall—which he overcompensated for by working out.

"I need it to win the championship game against Western next week," Jayden said. I could hear the urgency in his voice as he pulled on the drawstring of his bright blue varsity baseball hoodie.

Jay-Thor? Where had I heard that before? Oh right, that's what they chanted during the pep rallies and every time Jayden went up to bat. Most school sports were not high on my priority list — I considered it a win if I survived gym class — but even I had heard about Jayden's lightning baseball bat–aka Thor.

The corners of my mouth lifted as I thought about baseball. Mom had been a huge fan of the sport, always taking me to Texas Ranger games. She knew I wasn't anywhere close to being a baseball aficionado, but she'd insisted I attend the games with her. It was something she'd done with her dad, and she'd said attending games with me kept the tradition going.

"It's not funny! Without Thor, I keep striking out," Jayden whined, his voice nudging my thoughts back to his dilemma.

Jayden and I had been friends back in elementary school, but that all changed once we hit middle school, and Jayden became the star player of the baseball team. Thanks to his lucky lightning bat, this season, he'd been on a winning streak, hitting home runs every time he had been up to bat.

"You do stink without it," Kyle said, once again sending the table into laughter.

"Why is it called Thor again?" I heard a cheerleader ask.

"Oh, not this again, the magic bat made from a tree struck by the god Thor himself," Kyle smirked.

"Hey, doofus, how do you know that's not how the lightning mark got there?" Jayden chided, sitting upright in his chair. "I'm never going to win Andy's bet now. Heck, we probably won't even win the championship."

"Maybe someone will find it and return it," a different cheerleader said.

"Let's hope. I'll owe them big time." Jayden said, biting his nails.

I almost fell backward off the seat as the light bulb switched on in my head. This was my way in. I'd watched just about every detective show on television, especially the British ones on PBS. *Sherlock* was my favorite, and my mom and I had never missed *Midsomer Murders* on Friday nights. We'd compete to see who could spot the murderer first. I usually won.

I couldn't bear another year like the last one, constantly being ridiculed and bullied by Christian and the rest of the bros for being too girly. Seeing how the untouchables had just banded together to protect Jayden from Christian was proof that they would do the same for me if I were part of their fam.

A few of them sought me out when they needed help writing a paper or wanted to cheat off me during a test, but as soon as they got what they wanted, they went right back to ignoring me. But that was a thousand times better than the bros, who treated me like gum on the bottom of their shoe.

Finding Thor was way bigger than homework. If I solved the case, Jayden would surely show his gratitude by allowing me to hang with him and his friends. He had just said he would owe that person. Their validation would move me to the top of the school hierarchy. No more eating lunch in the far corner of the caf. No more jokes, jibes, or snickers about me being gay. It would change everything.

Plus, not only would I be putting my detective skills to use, but I would also be helping Jayden excel at Mom's favorite sport. This couldn't be a coincidence. Just as I suspected, Mom was watching over me, and she was giving me my chance to worm my way into the untouchables. That was the only way I was going to survive middle school.

I shuddered with excitement. I needed to channel my inner *Sherlock* and immediately start working the case.

CHAPTER 2

THE LEADOFF

Employing Sherlock's foolproof protocol, the first step was always questioning those closest to the victim. So, who better to start with than with Jayden's bestie, Kyle? I didn't know him well, but something about him always made me uber nervous anytime I was around him.

Jayden had jetted from the table to meet the coach, so this was the perfect time to talk to Kyle without raising any suspicion. I didn't want Jayden to know I was looking for the bat just yet, at least not until I had a promising lead. The worst thing that could happen would be getting his hopes up and then failing to find that bat. That would certainly ruin my chances of becoming an Untouchable.

I took a long, deep breath resummoning the courage I'd conjured before. I'd never really had a civil conversation with Kyle, so I wasn't sure how he would respond. He hadn't attended the same elementary school as Jayden and me, so I didn't know much about him other than he'd been voted MVP on the football team for the past two years. I had gym with him last year, but I barely attended, thanks to teacher-excused absences.

I stood up and approached the table to find Kyle chatting it up with Kushaela Collins, who was all over him as usual. As my grandmother, aka Big Momma, would say, everyone and their mother knew she liked him. If Jayden was the Big Man on Campus (BMOC), then as head cheerleader, Kushaela was easily his female counterpart. She was also one of the few African Americans in the untouchables' clique, proving there was hope for me.

Kushaela noticed me first. She smiled. "Hey, Evan, what's up? Did you finish that report for Texas history?" She was also the only untouchable who treated me with some shred of respect. We'd been in Gifted and Talented — or GT as we called them — classes together since elementary school. I was sure, if no one else, I could get her vote to become part of the group.

I nodded and opened my mouth to respond when Kyle tilted his head back, looking up at me. "Evan, just the person I wanted to see."

My stomach rumbled with dread as he pulled out the now vacant chair next to him. Why on earth would he want to talk to me? I ignored the looks of bewilderment and curious chatter all around us and looked right into Kyle's eyes. They were even bluer than I remembered. I felt as if I was being washed up in an enormous wave that engulfed me and smothered my breath.

"I've heard you're really good in English," Kyle said, snapping me back into reality. My face flamed as I sat down and tried to regain my train of thought.

"Duh. He's a walking dictionary," Andy Faulkner interjected, fiddling with the ends of his shoulder-length blond locks. He could never be accused of the same. Andy was the epitome of the dumb jock stereotype. I couldn't count the number of papers I'd written for him. At least he paid well.

I ignored him and continued looking into Kyle's sky blues, letting the waves wash over me as butterflies fluttered frantically in my stomach. He was actually being nice to me. What was more bewildering was why I relished it so much. I quivered, realizing I liked it a bit too much. I needed to refocus on the case. "Um . . . yeah, I guess so."

"Andy here told me how you helped him out. I was wondering if you could do me a solid."

"Uh . . ." I should have known he wanted something. "What do you need?"

"I need to write an essay about the three major themes in *Romeo and Juliet.*"

"Oh yeah, I can help you out with that. I did that assignment last year."

"Of course you did." Kyle smiled.

"When is it due? You want to meet in the library during lunch tomorrow to get started on it?" That would be the perfect time to ask him about Jayden's bat. I'd have him all to myself. Why was I more elated about the latter than the former in that scenario? *No, stop it!* I promised myself I wasn't going to have those kinds of thoughts anymore. It wasn't right. At least that's what everyone told me.

He lowered his voice and leaned toward me, causing my pulse to quicken. "Maybe you can just start it for me, and I can just look it over Monday morning before it's due to double-check for any changes." He winked.

My face fell. Of course. He was just like the others. He had no intention of actually writing any portion of that paper. He wanted me to do it all. If that was how it was going to be, then I better play along and go ahead and ask my questions about Thor.

"Sure, that can work." I cleared my throat, looking around. "So . . . I guess Jayden's pretty upset about his bat."

"Yeah, he's probably looking for it right now." Kyle snickered.

"Do you have any idea who took it?"

"Not a clue. But after that display," he gestured to the center of the caf, "Jay thinks it was Christian. They've always had a hard-on for each other."

I winced at the mention of Christian. To say we had a contentious relationship would be an understatement. It would not be at all surprising if he were the one behind the theft. "On the day the bat went missing, did you notice Christian acting suspiciously?"

"No more than usual. He's always a butthead." Kyle shrugged.

"Because, duh, Christian's a big, fat idiot," Kushaela said, jumping back into the conversation.

Kyle continued, "Although I think he left practice early or something on Monday, and Jay had the bat up until we jumped in the showers, so I don't think it was him."

I grimaced, thinking that lead was dead, but then I realized something. "But when you went into the showers, you couldn't see the lockers, right?"

"Yeah, that's right."

"So, he could have come back and taken the bat?"

"Hmm, I didn't think about that. I guess so."

"Did you notice anything anomalous that day?"

Kyle twisted his nose. "Ano-what?"

"Weird or out of the ordinary," I rephrased.

Kyle looked down, his brows furrowed. "You know what? Now that I think about it, when I came out of the shower, someone was standing next to Jayden's locker." He paused, frowning.

"Who was it?" I asked.

"It was Lammy, Lammy Hoang. He was standing right next to the locker. When we walked in, he looked all sus and then ran out of the locker room. I didn't think anything of it at the time. The dude's weird, but now I would say his behavior was, what did you say . . . anomalous?" Kyle raised an eyebrow.

My face flushed yet again. I honestly hadn't expected Kyle to be so approachable. I leaned in closer to him, my nostrils filling with oak, vanilla, and orange scents. Wow, he even smelled good.

I wriggled in the chair, bringing my attention back to finding the bat. Now there was yet another suspect. Maybe this case wasn't going to be as easy to solve as I'd thought it would be.

"Why are you so interested in the bat?" Kushaela said while wrinkling her nose.

Blimey! I knew that question was going to come up.

"Yeah, why do you care?" Kyle probed.

"Just curious," I said, leaning back. "It just sucks he doesn't have it, especially with the game against Western coming up." I'd better make my exit before they asked any more questions. My shoulders dropped. I hated to leave. How often did I get invited to sit down with the popular kids in the cafeteria? *Never.* Besides, I hated to admit it, but talking to Kyle was sending warm currents throughout my body.

Kushaela smiled. "I hear you. Jay needs that bat. Lightning or not, he's fire when he uses it. It's the only shot we have at winning the championship next week."

"Someone better find it and soon because Jay-Thor is quickly becoming Jay-sucks," Kyle smirked. "Last night's game was beyond sad."

As I stood up, Kyle said, "Don't forget the paper is due on Monday. Later, E."

Suddenly, a weird sensation in my stomach caught me off guard. No one at school called me E except for Angelica. Only close friends and family had that privilege. But for some odd reason, I didn't seem to mind Kyle calling me by my preferred alias. It certainly beat Sissy Sinclair.

I pushed the twinge in my gut away and refocused my attention on the case. I knew Lammy Hoang and exactly where he would be at that moment.

CHAPTER 3

THE BATBOY

In a mad dash, I ran from the cafeteria, through the corridor, and down the back stairs to the front gym entrance. I barreled through the double doors and was immediately welcomed with the odor of sweat mixed with disinfectant, which is what all gyms smelled like to me. I avoided the gym at all costs, and that included my own gym class. I would find any excuse to get out of it. Normally, I would offer to assist other teachers during that time, like helping Coach Zentell clean the beakers in the life science lab or Mrs. Dorsey wash the whiteboards in math class. All they had to do was write a note to Coach Green, stating they needed my assistance, and it counted as an excused absence. Unfortunately, I'd done it so much they'd started to catch on, so now they only did it on the rare occasions when they really needed my help with a project.

I walked around the bleachers to the storage closet, where I found Lammy stacking up the basketballs. Lam was his given Vietnamese name, but everyone called him Lammy. He was obsessed with sports and wanted to play all of them, but sadly, much like me, he wasn't particularly good at any of them. That's probably why we'd always been somewhat friendly with one another. Unlike me, though, Lammy was eager to be part of the teams in any way he could, so he had become the water boy for the football team, the towel boy for the basketball and soccer teams, and the batboy for the baseball team. One of his other duties was organizing the gym equipment in the storage area, which I knew he did just before my gym class right after lunch.

I tapped him on his shoulder. "Hey, Lammy, you busy?"

I startled him, causing him to knock down the basketballs he had just stacked up. "Geez, Evan."

Lammy was short and stocky, with dark black hair flowing down almost to his shoulders. He was dressed in his usual knee-length gym shorts and concert T-shirt. The mess I had created was causing Lammy to breathe heavily as he scampered across the floor, chasing the balls now rolling aimlessly all around us.

"Sorry about that." I scrambled around, helping him gather them up.

"What are you doing here?" Lammy asked as he started restacking them.

"I wanted to ask you about Jayden's missing bat."

"Thor is still missing?" He turned around to see me nod. "Bummer."

"Yeah, it is. I heard you were at practice on Monday when it went missing."

"Yeah, I was . . . What of it?" He stopped and looked at me.

"I heard you were right by his locker when he put it in there and then headed to the showers."

"Are you accusing me of something?" Lammy's jaw tightened, and his voice turned defensive.

I sensed Lammy getting huffy. I had to defuse the situation, and fast. "Look, Lammy, I know you had nothing to do with it. Someone just mentioned you were there and might have seen something." I'd seen Poirot use this technique numerous times, and it usually always got the suspect to spill the beans, as Big Momma would say.

Lammy closed the storage door and scampered toward me. I couldn't tell if he was angry and wanted to punch me for even insinuating he might have had something to do with the theft, so I shrank back. Bollocks! Maybe the Poirot approach didn't work.

Lammy stopped just in front of me and whispered, "Lowkey, I did see something, but you have to promise you won't say it came from me."

I exhaled. It worked, after all. Poirot didn't let me down. "C'mon, how long have we known each other? You can trust me."

The correct answer was over seven years since kindergarten, but rather than say that, he just gave me a quick nod and said, "Okay. After everyone went into the showers, I went back outside to grab the rest of the bases, and when I came back, Coach Bennett was standing right in front of Jayden's locker."

"What was he doing?" I asked, my curiosity piqued.

"Don't know. He took off as soon as I walked in."

"Did you see him take anything?"

"Nope. But before he left, he gave me this weird look. I took it as 'keep your mouth shut.' So I just got out of there." He sounded genuine. No wonder Kyle had said Lammy had been acting peculiar after the bat had been stolen.

Lammy glanced around the room, making sure everything was in its place before turning back to me. "Why are you asking about the bat? Did Jayden ask you to help him find it or something?"

Oh no, I didn't want this getting back to Jayden. "Umm . . . No. I'm just worried about the game. I just want us to win the championship next week," I stammered.

"Is that right?" Lammy looked at me suspiciously. "Since when do you care about sports, especially baseball?"

He wasn't buying it. I knew it was time to come clean. "Look, I'm trying to do Jayden a solid by finding the bat, but he doesn't know about it. I don't want to get his hopes up and then not deliver; you know what I mean?"

Lammy nodded. "I get it."

"So I will keep your secret if you keep mine."

The bell rang, signaling the end of lunch, just in time.

"Deal." Lammy held out his fist. I awkwardly stuck out mine, completing the fist bump.

"Okay, I gotta run," Lammy yelled over his shoulder as he ran out the door. "I do hope you find it. Jayden is an okay dude, but he's an awesome player when he has Thor. Now that dweeb Andy Falkner is getting all the hits."

I could only imagine how mortified Jayden must be to lose his cred to Andy. Talk about cutthroat competitors. I hustled from the gym, hoping I could get to the library before the lunch period ended. If I was going to take on this case, I would need some assistance, and I knew the perfect person for the job.

CHAPTER 4

THE FIRST INNING

"You're straight-up crazy." Angelica tipped back in her seat, kicking her red Nike high-top against the table leg. Despite her pale skin, freckles, and frizzy red hair, I was astonished at how she always acted blacker than me.

Almost everyone in the library turned to look at us, including the librarian, Mrs. Harlin (or Mrs. Harwitch, as most students called her). She glided over to us. In her late twenties and dressed like she should be walking down the runway at a fashion show, Mrs. Harlin was far from the stereotypical buttoned-up, rigid librarian. Yet, she still didn't tolerate any mischief in her library.

"Everything OK here, Mr. Sinclair and Ms. Tyler?" she asked with a look of concern more than anger. Fortunately, Angelica and I were regulars at the library, so she had a soft spot for us. Between dealing with the horrors of middle school and what had happened with Mom, libraries had become my sanctuaries when things had gotten really bad last year. I liked the smell and the feeling of being surrounded by books; it always put me at ease. Within the pages of all these books, there were so many adventures to choose from, which fascinated me.

"Fine, Mrs. Harlin," I said, quickly plopping down into a chair opposite Angelica.

"All good, Mrs. Harlin," Angelica said with a smile as she sat back down, tucking one of her red curls behind her ear.

Mrs. Harlin's face softened. "Just keep it down." She walked back to her desk in the center of the room. The school library didn't have a robust catalog of books. It was just a single large room with ten-foot-tall bookcases lining the walls and a bunch of tables and chairs in the center.

Angelica wasted no time getting back on topic. "That bogus Thor bat?" Angelica waved her finger. "Why would you help him? He's always been a little sus. Remember when he asked you for help last year with his research paper and ended up making you write the entire thing? C'mon, E, don't be basic."

"Basic? Oh great, you've been watching *The Real Housewives* again," I said, rolling my eyes. She never missed an episode.

"That's better than those boring English shows you watch." She placed her hand back on her hip. I smiled, thinking back to when I had invited her over to binge-watch *Midsomer Murders,* and she'd fallen asleep during the first episode.

"Yeah, OK, Jayden has manipulated me in the past, but this is different," I said, not sure who I was trying to convince more, her or myself. "Without his bat, his reputation is on the line, so the stakes are much higher. He'd be much more amenable if I got Thor back."

Angelica shrugged her shoulders. "Whatever. You're so thirsty to hang out with those conceited douchebags."

"I'm not thirsty," I said a little too emphatically. Thanks to her reality-TV addiction, she was constantly schooling me on the hippest slang. Her fascination with talking like a streetwise reality star has caused her to be the butt of almost as many jokes as me. It's also why she no longer hangs out with the untouchables. "I admit they can be pernicious, but they aren't that bad." Okay, that wasn't exactly true. Some of them were pretty bad, but once I was in the tribe, that would change.

Angelica rolled her eyes. "Perni-what? You and your wackadoo words."

If I had a dollar for every time someone commented on the way I talked, from vocabulary and pitch to inflection, I would be a millionaire.

Angelica cracked a small smile before getting back to the matter at hand. "Even if you do get his ridiculous bat back, you don't actually think they'll let you hang out with them? They're just going to use you to help them with their homework and then continue to call you a big gay nerd behind your back."

"Really, Ang?" I cringed, taking a step back.

"Sorry, not sorry. 'Jay-Thor' doesn't deserve your help.'" She used air quotes around Jayden's nickname. "None of them do."

I expected this response from her. After her falling out with a few of the untouchables, she'd constantly cautioned me against trying so hard to join their pack. But things were different for her. They weren't calling her gayboy and Sissy Sinclair every school day.

That would all change if I could hitch my wagon, as Big Momma often said, to the untouchables; it would make my life so much easier. No one would make fun of me or feel sorry for the boy whose mother had died. I would finally be at the top of the social food chain. More importantly, I would finally fit in and be a regular normal kid.

Despite Angelica's objections, I knew she was the one person who would always be in my corner. And at some point during my investigation, I was sure I was going to need her help. While she was no longer part of the untouchables, she still had access to some popular kids that I didn't. "I know you don't like them, but this is important to me." I tilted my head down and looked up at her, showing her my big, brown, puppy-dog eyes. "Will you help me?"

She took a beat and just looked at me. "I will never understand why, but you're my fam, and you're going to need someone to have your back when they kick you to the curb."

It wasn't exactly the support I was hoping for, but it would do. "Thanks, Ang."

"Just know I am doing this for you, not for them," she said, rolling her neck.

I smiled. "Understood."

The bell rang, signaling the end of lunch. As I walked to class, I attempted to sort out all the clues from the interviews with Kyle and Lammy that were now whirling in my mind. Once school ended, I was going to talk to the one person who could help me sort them all out.

CHAPTER 5

THE WINDUP

My heart almost beat out of my chest as I flew down the road like I was racing in the Tour de France on my emerald green, 21-speed mountain bike. I had just gotten it for my birthday, so I was still breaking it in, but it was way better than Dad's hand-me-down ten-speed I had before.

Out of breath, I threw open the squeaky screen door and rushed into Big Momma's house. "Big Momma? It's me. Are you here?" I gasped, sucking in as much air as I could between every other word.

The aroma of coffee infused the house as usual. It smelled woody and burned, but that was just the way Big Momma liked it.

Big Momma stood at the sink in one of her many multicolored, lavishly jeweled kimonos, washing the dishes. A few strands of her short gray hair hung in front of her face. She only stood at four feet, eight inches tall, but Dad said her mouth alone was big enough for two women.

"There you are. I was yelling for you," I said as I walked into the kitchen.

"I heard you, and you know better than coming into the house and yelling like that. You can wait until you see me and then speak politely."

That was Big Momma. She was all about decorum. Dad said she acted that way because she worked over 30 years for an uppity white doctor who was too liberal for his own good. Whatever that meant.

I cocked my head to the side, slightly irritated I couldn't get right to my news. "Uh . . . hello, Big Momma, how are you doing today?"

"Cheers, Evan." Her light-brown eyes glittered in the sunlight beaming through the window over the kitchen sink.

"Nice one." It tickled me to hear Big Momma using British lingo after only watching a few shows. Over the past few months, I had introduced her to some of my favorite British mysteries. So far, her favorite was *Miss Marple*, although she said Miss Marple was too much of a busybody, and if she didn't mind her own business, she would be the one killed.

It wasn't quite the same as watching them with Mom. Big Momma liked to ask a lot of questions during the show, which had been a no-no for Mom and me. But spending time with Big Momma reminded me of how similar Mom's mannerisms were to her mother's, which comforted me, especially in the months just after mom's death.

"I'm just fine. How are you getting along?"

I jumped at the chance to finally share my big news. "I'm going to find Jayden Stevens' missing lightning bat."

"Is that so?" She placed her hand on her hip. "First of all, what the heck is a lightning bat, and secondly, who in the dickens is Jayden Stevens?"

I decided to answer the second question first. It was easier to explain. "Jayden is the most popular guy in school. He pretty much calls the shots for the untouchables," I gushed.

Big Momma stuck out her bottom lip, unimpressed. "So tell me this – what does any of this have to do with you?"

"Big Momma, I told you I want to be a police detective, like McGarrett on *Hawaii Five-O*." That was one of the few shows I watched with my dad. Well, when he was around, which wasn't very often as of late.

"Do you also want to be shot at? Because that is part of the job too. You do know you have to be a policeman first."

"Only until I pass the detective's exam." I would not be deterred.

"One day as a policeman is long enough to get shot," Big Momma said sternly. She sighed. "My goodness, what would your mother say? Lord rest her soul." Big Momma sighed again.

I looked up at the ceiling. The mention of Mom sent shivers down my spine, reminding me how much I missed her. "Mom always encouraged my sleuthing. And she'd love that I was helping someone find a baseball bat."

Big Momma paused, looking away. "She did love baseball, just like your Big Daddy." She turned back to face me. "What happened to you becoming a chef?"

I folded my arms. "That was back when I was in second grade."

"Is it because your dad said cooking was for girls?" Big Momma's lips tightened. "Don't listen to him. I told you the most successful and popular chefs are men."

That was part of the reason. I was already being called a sissy boy, so the last thing I wanted was to add fuel to the flames, but I didn't want to tell Big Momma that. I looked down and, in a low whisper, said, "I just enjoyed cooking with Mom."

Big Momma's face softened. "I know you did." She put her hand on my shoulder. "I miss her too. Every single day."

As I fought the tears beginning to form in the corners of my eyes, Big Momma poured us each a cup of coffee and brought it over to the barstools where I had already parked myself. I drank it black, just like Big Momma. Dad would never allow me to drink coffee at home. It was one of his countless commandments. No coffee. No smoking. Fortunately, the coffee rule didn't exist at Big Momma's. "No coffee. Why that's poppycock," I remembered Big Momma saying to Mom when she'd learned about my dad's restrictions. "Evan's an old soul. What else would he drink?" I wasn't exactly sure what that meant but based on the difficulty I had connecting with most people my age, I'd come to believe it wasn't a compliment.

At least I had Big Momma. She had always understood me in ways the rest of my family didn't, even if she didn't approve of my current career aspirations.

As she set the coffee in front of me, she asked calmly, "Have you texted your dad yet?"

Oh, crikey! "Thanks for reminding me. I completely forgot." I pulled out my phone and typed a quick text.

At Big Mommas.

"Evan, you know better than that. You know how he is." Big Momma's voice turned stern again.

Oh, did I ever! Dad had turned into a total control freak over the past year, requiring me to check in with him whenever I changed locations. So annoying! Something about wanting to know where I was at all times. The worst was that whenever I forgot, he'd have a complete meltdown.

My phone chimed, signaling Dad's response.

About time. I was wondering where you were. Why does it take so long for you to get there? We need to talk about this tonight.

I frowned and then took a long, deep breath.

"Hang in there, kiddo," Big Momma said, placing her hand on my back. "If he spent more time with you, he wouldn't need you to text him all the doggone time," Big Momma quipped as she sat on the barstool next to me. It was no secret that Big Momma thought Dad's priorities were in the wrong place. "But that's another story. So back to this lightning bat, what is it, and do you have any idea who would want to take it?"

I took a sip of the strong, nutty coffee before replying, "He calls the bat Thor because it is supposedly made from a tree that was struck by Thor's lightning bolt. That's why it's lucky. It even has a lightning bolt carved on the handle."

Big Momma's jaw dropped. "You're kidding me?"

"I know. It's ridiculous. They even call him Jay-Thor and chant his name when he's up to bat."

Big Momma raised her eyebrows. "Jay-Thor? Really?"

"Now you see what I have to deal with every day. They are Neanderthals." I chuckled. "They believe anything."

"I don't know if that's true, but it sounds like this bat is kind of like a security blanket. It gives him the confidence he needs to do well. There's nothing wrong with that. At times, we could all use that kind of magic."

I got what Big Momma was saying, but at the moment, I didn't have time to worry about the supposed magical powers of an inanimate object. I had a case to solve. "Anyway, I already questioned his best friend and the team's batboy today, but it was mostly for reconnaissance. I just wanted to ascertain if they saw anything the day the bat went missing. I think the prime suspect is a kid named Christian. He's been jealous of Jayden all season."

"And why is that?"

"Jayden's been hitting home runs all season, stealing the spotlight. Maybe he thought taking it would ruin Jayden's batting average, or maybe he thought the bat would bring him luck."

"Any of those things happen?"

"Yes and no. Without Thor, Jayden's batting average plummeted, but Christian hasn't become the team's new power hitter, so if he does have it, the bat's supposed mojo is not working for him."

"So when are you going to talk to this boy Christian?"

I winced. "I don't know. He hates me, so I doubt he'll even talk to me."

"Then maybe you need to approach him in a different way."

"What do you mean?" I asked.

"Well, you said he doesn't like Jayden. Maybe he would be willing to talk to someone with whom he had something in common."

"But I don't have anything in common with him." I was completely confused.

"That might be true, but he doesn't know that."

"Know what?" I asked, still confused, until it finally hit me. Duh, of course. I must make him think we have something in common.

"Nothing brings two people together more than having a common enemy," Big Momma drilled in her point.

I raised my eyebrows. "Do you think that would work for Coach Bennett too? The batboy, Lammy, spotted him beside the locker just before the bat went missing."

Big Momma set her coffee down on the bar. "You think an adult might have taken it?"

"In the words of Hercule Poirot, 'I suspect everybody till the last minute,'" I said, pointing my finger in the air. Agatha Christie's *Murder on the Orient Express* was one of my favorite murder mysteries.

Big Momma laughed. "Talking to adults is no different from talking to your friends. They think it is all about them, and they love to talk about themselves, especially if you can give them a reason to."

I scratched my head. "Big Momma, that doesn't make any . . ." Wait. All I had to do was make him think I was interested.

I got up and hugged Big Momma. "What would I ever do without you?" As I asked the question, I realized I hadn't just meant in this instance but during the horrific past year.

"Let's hope you don't find out anytime soon. Now, work this DVR for me so I can go back and see what I missed on *Wheel*."

I grabbed the remote and rewound the program for her.

"Thank you. I can never work that durn thingamajig. I don't know what I would do without you."

I smiled, handed her the control, and sat back down to watch *Wheel of Fortune.*

CHAPTER 6

THE POP-UP

Pre-game time! I switched on my playlist and popped in my earbuds as I plopped into a chair at an empty table. After Mom had passed, I'd been beginning every school morning in the library with music and solitude before enduring the hell known as middle school.

Softly humming Blake Shelton's "Neon Light," I took a bite of my croissant and closed my eyes, attempting to shut out the world at least for a few seconds. When I opened my eyes, I almost choked on my breakfast as I looked up to see Jayden and Kyle enter the library. What were they doing here? They never came into the library, at least not voluntarily. Jayden nodded at Mrs. Harlin, who gave them both a stern look and her typical, "Shh."

Jayden patted my shoulder as he and Kyle sat on either side of me. "So what is all this I'm hearing about you asking questions about my bat?" Jayden said, obviously not interested in small talk.

My mouth fell open. I cleared my throat. "Um . . ." I rose to my feet, trying to find the right words to explain myself.

Jayden raised his eyebrows and smiled. "Blake Shelton, huh?" he snickered, recognizing the song spewing out of my earbuds, which had fallen out of my ears when I'd stood and were now resting on the table. "You're the only black bruh I know who likes country music."

I wasn't sure how to respond. Comments like that got under my skin, but sadly I was used to it. Living in the western suburbs of Fort Worth, there weren't very many students who looked like me. I was often the only African American in my GT classes, which meant I often got called out for doing things that African Americans supposedly didn't do. Even Dad constantly chided me for listening to country music instead of jazz, which was his music of choice.

I bit my tongue. Jayden Stevens was the guy everyone in school aspired to be or, at the very least, hang with, which was exactly what

I wanted, so I figured I better play it cool. "This is Texas. A lot of people like country music."

"I don't." Jayden cocked his head to the side. "So, did you take Thor?" Jayden asked, getting back on topic.

"Of course not. What would I want with a baseball bat?" I said, taken aback.

"It's a lucky lightning bat; let's not forget," Kyle jived.

Jayden turned to address Kyle. "And how many hits have I gotten this season compared to you? My record speaks for itself."

"Before or after your precious bat was taken? Because your stats aren't doing any talking now," Kyle laughed.

"Shut up, it's not funny," Jayden said, sticking out his bottom lip.

I just sat there watching the exchange, happy it had taken the attention off me.

"So you never answered me. Why are you asking questions about Thor?"

"I'm worried about the championships next week. I know if you had the bat, Western wouldn't have a chance, so I just thought maybe I could help figure out who took it," I said, hoping he would buy it.

Jayden didn't say a word as he glared at me. He finally said, "Bull. You don't give a crap about baseball."

Flummoxed, my heart felt like it was going to beat out of my chest. "My mom was a big baseball fan, so I was just trying to help. But fine, I'll stop." The last thing I wanted to do was ruin my chances of being an Untouchable.

Jayden's eyes suddenly grew larger. "No, I don't want you to stop."

"Huh?" I said, dumbfounded. *No way!* Does Jayden Stevens actually want my help?

Kyle's mouth flopped open. "You can't be serious? You think *he* can find your bat?"

Jayden grunted, glaring at Kyle. "Right now, he's a better friend than you are."

Kyle rolled his eyes. "He's a brainiac and all, but do you honestly think anyone would talk to him?" Kyle said as if I weren't sitting there.

"You did," Jayden said briskly. "Have I not asked the entire team for help? And none of you have done as much investigating as Evan, and he did it without being asked. I even asked Coach and Principal Albert to help me find it, and they both looked at me like I had two heads." His voice rose with each word.

"Boo-hoo, Lord forbid someone doesn't bow down to help the almighty Jayden," Kyle said with a sneer. I couldn't tell if he was being serious or playfully trying to rustle Jayden's feathers.

"Shh." Mrs. Harlin shot us her famous don't-make-me-come-over-there look.

Ignoring Mrs. Harlin and Kyle's last comment, Jayden's eyes suddenly lit up. "Hey, I just remembered that our boy Evan here has a knack for finding things. You remember when we were in scouts?" Jayden looked at me.

"You were in the *boy scouts*?" Kyle said, not at all hiding his disdain.

"Yeah, in third and fourth grades." His eyes sped to Kyle. "Don't ask."

I knew what he was referring to. A fellow scout had stolen Jayden's obstacle course medal. I identified a suspect and followed him to see him bury it under a tree. My old friend Patrick and I dug it up and returned it to Jayden before exposing the thief to the troop leader. My most vivid memory from that day, other than Jayden's gratitude, was the hug my mother had given me. She said, "Aren't you the clever one? I'm so proud of you." That was when I knew I wanted to be a detective.

"So you really want me to find your bat?" I asked louder than I meant to, eager with anticipation. I ignored all the eyes on me. I knew the library nerds were all wondering why two untouchables were sitting with a nobody like me.

"Tell you what, you find my bat, and I'll owe you, big time."

That's what I wanted to hear. "Really? Like how big?"

"You name it," Jayden said without hesitation.

"Like . . ." I knew that I couldn't ask him to instantly make me an untouchable, even he didn't have that kind of sway, and even if he did, it wouldn't be worth a hill of beans, as Big Momma often said, because my finding the bat would blackmail him into doing it. The group wouldn't have accepted me on their own accord, which was the entire point. I had to start small. Baby steps.

"Let me sit with you at lunch in the caf," I said without fully thinking it through, but that was the only thing that I could think of that was within Jayden's power to grant, allowing me the exposure I needed to infiltrate my way into the group.

"What? You gotta be crazy!" Kyle exclaimed, throwing his hands in the air.

Jayden looked toward the ceiling but didn't say anything right away. He put his finger up to his chin and then said, "Deal."

"Oh, great, wait until everyone hears about this," Kyle rebuked.

Jayden leaned toward Kyle. "If I get Thor back, then I don't give a crap what any of them think about Evan sitting with us. It's not like they are lining up to help me find it."

I broke into a smile. "Ok then, let's get down to business." I tried to sound cool but regretted it as soon as I said it. What I wanted to do was get up and dance a jig, but instead, I pulled a few sheets of paper from my binder to take notes.

Jayden sat back in his chair. "I think I can save you a lot of time because I know who took it. I just can't prove it."

Kyle shook his head. "Let me guess, Christian?"

"I keep telling you that birdbrain has it." Jayden clenched his teeth and turned to me. "Have you talked to him yet? He was salty at practice the other day and kept giving me dirty looks. I was about to get in his face."

Blimey! "But you didn't, right?" I tried not to sound annoyed.

Jayden folded his arms. "Naaw, but I wanted to. As I said, I don't have any proof."

I sighed, feeling relieved. Kyle jabbed Jayden with his elbow. "I think you should just jump him again and make him give it back."

"No, that's a bad idea," I said. "Right now, we need to let him think he's gotten away with it." In my detective shows, once a suspect thought they were in the clear, that was when they always made a mistake. "We all know how mercurial he can be. He might do something rash. It's much better to wait and let him incriminate himself. That way, we can catch him red-handed."

Kyle crossed his eyes. "Mercur-what?" he laughed. "Dang, you and your big, crazy words."

Jayden grinned. "Evan's like a walking encyclopedia. That's why I need him on the case."

I couldn't help but smile. "Mercurial just means unpredictable." My chest swelled with pride. I'd just received a compliment from Jayden Stevens, of all people. That was quite the twist, but I'd better get to the matter at hand so I could prove myself worthy of his praise. "I am talking with Coach Bennett during lunch because some things just aren't adding up."

"Really? You think the coach has something to do with it?" Kyle asked, his sky-blue eyes wide as saucers.

"I'm not sure, but at the very least, I think he might know something that could lead us to the thief." I didn't want to give too much away.

"He's been acting weird," Jayden said. "And he doesn't even care that Thor is missing. He acts like it's a joke or something." Jayden pulled at his tousled hair.

What an odd way for a coach to react, especially when it concerns his star player. "I will talk to Christian today. But please, neither of you do anything to upset him because then he'll just shut down, and we won't get any answers." Heck, I wasn't even sure Christian would give me the time of day, given our prickly relationship, but I had a secret weapon I planned on deploying.

Kyle made a face. "Yeah, okay. I won't say anything."

"Me neither. I just really want Thor back." Jayden's arrogance faded, making him almost sound sincere. "I gotta get out of this slump. I have to wipe that smug grin off Russell's face this year."

Kyle saw the confused look on my face. "Russell Harden. Western's team captain. He and Jayden have been frenemies since little league." He playfully jabbed Jayden's side. "I'm not going to lie; you do suck pretty bad without Thor."

"Shut up, douchebag." Jayden slapped Kyle on the head.

"I'll get it back. Just give me a little more time." I wasn't sure where all this confidence was coming from, but it was invigorating. Part of it was because I finally wasn't spending my lunch alone. I now sat with two of the most popular kids in the school. It wasn't in the lunchroom yet, but it was the first step. I wanted to stand up and do the two-step. High on my first exposure to being part of the in-crowd, I decided to take a chance.

"Hey, have you guys ever hung out at the downtown library? I go all the time. They have movies, music, and tons of cool stuff to do. I also ice-skate across the street at the Saeller Center. They even have a Bahama Buck's." Everybody in Texas knew they had the creamiest ice cream and juiciest snow cones in the state.

Jayden sniggered. "Nope, I can honestly say I've never done that. I've ice-skated at the center before, but the library always seemed boring to me."

"Yeah, me too." Kyle echoed Jayden's laughter.

My heart sank. Well, that hadn't gone well. I should have stopped while I was ahead.

Kyle shoved Jayden's shoulder. "Hey, if you don't get your bat back, you'll need something else to do. Could be fun. And E and I need to get to work on that flippin' Shakespeare paper, right, E?" He nodded at me before turning back to face Jayden. "Whaddaya think?"

My head tipped to the side. The Kyle from yesterday was back, and so were the pangs in my stomach as I stared at his dimples. I had honestly forgotten all about that paper, but even more startling, Kyle wanted to work on the paper together. I was certain he was just act-ing cool to me, so I would write the entire thing for him. Maybe he's not the total jerk Ang thought he was.

Jayden rolled his eyes. "What the heck, why not? I'm in if you are. But it better be hella fun."

The bell rang, signaling the end of lunch. Jayden got up. "Alright, man, I gotta get to class. Keep me posted on Thor, and call me to-morrow if you go to the library."

Kyle punched me on the shoulder a lot more lightly than he had Jayden. "Yeah, I gotta run too. I'm also down for the library thing if Jayden's going."

They were both gone before I could even reply. I couldn't contain my glee as I sat there beaming from ear to ear. The two most popular kids in school were going to hang out with me at the library tomor-row. As much as I hated to admit it, I was most excited about spending time with Kyle. I bit my lower lip, lowering my gaze.

"So, are they going to be in here before school every day now? If so, I'm going to have to find another place to chill." I swiveled around to see Angelica staring me down. I should have known she'd watched the entire exchange with Kyle and Jayden. Nothing happened in the library without her knowing about it.

"I still can't believe you're helping those nitwits find that phony bat," Angelica smirked. "You doing this to be their friend, or do you want something else?" She pursed her lips together.

"What are you talking about?" My face grew crimson as my eyes darted around the room. I had an idea of what she meant, but surely she wouldn't think of going there. "Guess who's hanging out with me at the downtown library this weekend?" I said, trying to change the subject.

She scoffed. "Jayden Stevens and Kyle Reynolds are spending a day with you at the library? You gotta be kidding."

"Yep." I folded my arms across my chest. "And for your information, Kyle doesn't want me to write his entire paper; he just wants some help with it."

Angelica raised her eyebrows and leaned toward me. "Uh-huh . . . You just want to spend the day with Kyle."

"What?" To even my surprise, my voice turned full soprano. "You know it's not like that." I frantically surveyed the room, confirming no one was listening. My heart started beating faster, and the room began to spin. How did she know? I hadn't told anyone about the funny feeling I had in my gut or how my pulse raced when I interacted with Kyle.

Angelica's face softened. "OK, OK. I believe you. But so what if you, as they say in those boring British shows you watch, fancied a boy? We visited a church in Meadowbrook where the minister said that all LGBTQ people were going to hell. Mom got up and made us all leave. She said life is too short to be surrounded by such hate. But anyway, if you were gay, just do me a favor and pick someone better than that poser Kyle."

Badmouthing "homosexuals," aka "abominations," as my minister often called them, was a typical Sunday at my church. I looked up into Angelica's polka-dot-freckled face. I was tempted to confide my confusion to her, but I couldn't find the words, and my heart was racing so fast that I thought it would pop right out of my chest. What was I doing? I had a case to solve. That's where my attention should be.

"I gotta go. I'm gonna be late for class." I frantically gathered my books from the table. "I'll catch ya later." I ran from the library without looking back.

.

CHAPTER 7

THE HOME STAND

As I walked into the locker room, I squinched my nose and was immediately greeted with the dank, dirty sock smell that always seemed to flood the confined space. I cringed, trying not to remember the many times I had been humiliated in this room. I did fairly well when it came to sports like archery and cross-country, but those weren't the ones that people cared about, and they certainly didn't make you popular. Much to my dad's consternation, I was completely inept at baseball, football, and basketball — which everyone assumed I should be good at because I was relatively tall, lanky, and African American.

I sucked up my trepidation and walked past the long row of bright blue lockers toward the back corridor. I told Coach Bennett I would interview him for the school newspaper during my lunch period. That had been the only cover I could think of using to ask him questions without creating suspicion.

The coaches' offices were behind the locker room. I'd just passed the lockers and entered the small waiting area, which consisted of two chairs and a small table outside the two coaching offices, when I heard someone shouting, "Listen, Bennett, you better settle up and fast, or I can't promise your safety."

The yeller's back was to me, but then he spun around, barreled down the hallway, and ran smack into me. My eyes closed upon impact as my head collided right into the bloke's chest, leading me to believe he was much taller than me. By the time I reopened my eyes, he was already down the hall and headed for the locker room door. I barely caught a glimpse of his face and couldn't discern anything specific, other than he was white, had short, sandy-colored hair, and was wearing a light gray suit.

Disoriented, I fell back against the wall, taking a few deep breaths to regain my bearings. Why was the guy in such a hurry? He hadn't even had the decency to ask me if I was OK, or at least say "excuse me" or "I'm sorry." As an adult, he should have known better. I shook off my confusion and continued to Coach Bennett's office.

Coach Bennett sat in his office behind his desk, looking distraught, his eyes narrowing as he focused very intently on the computer sitting in front of him. His hands trembled as he poked at the keyboard. I tapped on the half-opened door, still trying to catch my breath. "Coach Bennett . . ."

The coach looked up, almost cringing as he wiped the sweat glistening on his forehead before he quickly dropped his shoulders and smiled, realizing it was me and not the ill-mannered chap I'd just collided with. "Hey there, you must be Evan?" He nervously ran his hands through his unkempt, shoulder-length brown hair.

Coach Bennett was a skinny guy, about 5'8" and only weighing about 145 pounds soaking wet, as Big Momma would say. I'd always wondered how he had become a coach because he certainly didn't look the part.

"Yes. Uhm . . . Nice to meet you, Coach. Thanks for seeing me so quickly." Moisture began to form under my armpits.

"It's about time the newspaper did a story. We've been killing it. We are division champs, for Christ's sake." He forced a smile.

I looked down at my feet. "I agree, uhm . . . The paper should do a better job of, uhm, covering division-winning sports teams like, uhm, baseball."

My eyes blinked rapidly as I strained to organize my thoughts. Crud! I wasn't selling this interview. I channeled Detective Chief Inspector Barnaby in *Midsomer Murders*. I needed to mirror his confidence and charm.

I took a deep breath, then finally looked up, stared directly into the coach's eyes, and asked my next question, "So how long have you been with the team?"

"I coached a baseball team at my last school in Ohio right after I graduated from college, so when I was hired here to teach history, they asked me if I would also be interested in coaching the team here, and I jumped at the chance."

"So from Ohio to Texas. That must have been quite the change." I honestly didn't know anything about Ohio, but most people I met who weren't from Texas always said the Lone Star State was like no other.

"That's an understatement," the coach said with a smile. "But I have to say; I like it here. Plus, my sister, Jess, moved here a few years ago, and she is very active in the community and the church, so that has helped with the transition."

"Oh, nice. Do you know which church she attends?"

"She's Seventh-day Adventist, so she goes to the one on the south side."

My eyes lit up. "Oh, you mean Grace Temple. My grandmother goes there." I would never have guessed that. While my grandmother's church boasted a multiracial congregation, being located on the south side where the majority of African Americans lived, it included more black congregants than any others.

He leaned back in his chair. "Really? I've been a couple times. My wife loves it. It seems like church is a big deal down here. One of the first questions I get asked when I meet someone is, 'Where do you go to church?'"

"Oh, you have no idea," I said, trying to hide my disdain. I had a love-hate relationship with church for too many reasons to list. "I go to church with my grandmother sometimes, so maybe I'll see you there."

Maybe his wife was African American? I looked around for any family pictures on his desk, but all I saw were baseball plays scrawled on graph paper and what looked like travel brochures with casinos on them. I think they were for Las Vegas because I recognized the hotel shaped like a pyramid. Luxor, I think it was. We stayed there once during one of our many family vacations in Vegas. Dad would play those slot machines for hours on end. I loved going to the glitzy acrobatic shows. The staging and the way they contorted their bodies were unbelievable.

"Do you play any sports? I'm also going to be coaching basketball in the spring."

I grunted. Why did everyone assume that I wanted to or even could play basketball? Not all African-American boys wanted to dribble a ball. "Nope, not my thing." I raised my hand, sticking my pen up in the air. "I'll stick with writing."

"To each their own, but I think every boy should play a sport." I heard the familiar disappointment in his voice. It sounded just like Dad's.

"I do cross-country in the fall."

"Not quite the same, but I guess it's better than nothing," the coach smirked.

I tightened my grip on the pen, almost snapping it in two. *Enough small talk.* "So, what do you think about the baseball team here?"

"I think they are a great group of guys who have a lot of potential. I'm excited to see how they're gonna perform this season."

"Are there any standout players?" I asked, grinning inside. I'd finally hit my stride and was gearing up to ask the real questions.

"Yes, a few. Kyle Reynolds, Christian Carlson, Andy Falkner, and of course, Jayden Stevens . . . He's got a mean swing on him."

I moved in for the kill. "But I've heard Jayden's lightning bat is missing, and his performance has been suffering because of it. Is there any truth to that?"

The coach scratched his head then quickly placed his hands on his desk. "For Christ's sake, not that *Thor* bat again. Yes, there have been some hiccups with that, but he just needs more confidence. He's the one with the skills. He doesn't need some special bat," he said with a half-hearted snicker.

"Even if it's not supernatural, it does give Jayden a boost of confidence, allowing him to play well. I would think, as a coach, you would find that to be important."

"I mean . . . well . . . of course, it's important in that sense . . . but it's just a bat. I know everyone has bought into it being something like Thor's hammer. That's fun and all, but there is nothing special about it." He folded his arms. "Jayden just needs to learn how to hone his skills without a crutch."

It was time. I asked the ten-million-dollar question. "Were you at practice Monday, the day it was stolen?"

"Uh . . . I don't believe so. Hmm . . . I had to leave early that day."

Lammy had said the coach had been there that day. Why would Coach Bennett lie about it? I decided to let that go for the moment. "I heard Jayden and Christian have a beef. Maybe he could have had something to do with the bat's disappearance?"

"I don't believe anyone on the team had anything to do with it. Yes, those two have had their altercations, but competition is a healthy part of sportsmanship. I teach all of the players that team-work always comes first before petty disagreements."

"Jayden was getting all the attention, and now the spotlight has switched to Christian. So, perhaps jealousy could be the cause of the bat's disappearance."

"I wouldn't say Christian is the only one in the spotlight. Andy is getting a lot of hits too. I mean, they're all good players, lucky bats or not." The coach suddenly stopped himself, furrowed his brows, and stared directly into my eyes, causing my heart to jump. "For Christ's sake, I thought this interview was about the team's season, not a lucky bat."

Oops, I better back off. "Of course, it's about the team. I was just curious, that's all," I said, trying to laugh off the nervousness that was flooding over me. "So, let's get back to the team stats. They've changed quite a bit since you've been here."

I forced myself to smile and pretend I was paying attention as the coach droned on about how the changes he had made were respon-sible for the team's improvement, but I was barely listening to a single word he was saying. Why had the coach lied about him being in the locker room just before the bat had been stolen?

Finally, the coach stopped yammering and said, "Yeah . . . So, with those adjustments, I think we have a great shot at the championships this year."

I could tell the interview was coming to an end, so I decided to make one last-ditch effort to get the information I needed. "Do you think that can be done without Jayden's bat, even if it's just a crutch?"

"Without a doubt. He just needs to stop focusing on the bat and focus on his skills instead."

"You think he can do that? The bat seems pretty important to him."

"There's nothing special about that bat. It's ridiculous that he and all his friends are making such a big deal out of it." He slit his eyes at me, causing the hairs on my neck to stand on edge. "He should just pick up another bat and make it as lucky as the one he lost." He slithered back into his chair. "It'll turn up, eventually."

I knew Coach Bennett was getting suspicious, but I had to pry just a little more. "And you said you weren't there the day it was taken?"

"I don't believe so, but then again, I'm not sure when the bat was taken."

"Last Monday."

"Oh, right . . . I'm pretty sure I left right after practice. The Little League team I coach had a game that day."

"Hmm, that is strange because I know a few of the players said they saw you in the locker room just before going into the showers."

"Um . . . well . . . maybe . . . as I said, I don't exactly remember. Wait, how did we get back on the bat thing?" He sat upright and rubbed his nose furiously, almost as if he was trying to remove it from his face.

His behavior signaled to me that it was time to back off. "Sorry, my journalistic curiosity got the better of me again. Anyway, thank you, Coach, for taking the time to chat with me. I better get back so I can write up the story."

I pretended not to hear the coach ask when the story would be out as I closed the door and bolted out of the locker room.

CHAPTER 8

THE FOUL BALL

Christian was in my homeroom, so, unfortunately, I knew him better than I would have liked. I deliberately steered clear of him because he loved to make me the punch line of most of his jokes, which usually sent the entire classroom into hysterical laughter. His dad worked in construction, so when he wasn't talking about baseball, then it was about building something. I remembered him saying he had been around tools since he was in diapers. He was part of the theater stage crew helping build the set for the school's spring production of *Grease*, so I wasn't surprised to find him in the shop classroom right after school.

I walked into the shop, dragging Angelica behind me. She had reluctantly agreed to accompany me to talk to Christian, but it had taken some serious convincing on my part. I had to agree to binge-watch a full season of *Love and Hip Hop*, which I loathed, but having her come along would be worth it. Christian had a thing for her, so I needed to use that to my advantage. "Geez, Evan, that was in fifth grade," Angelica had protested. But if I wanted to get Christian to talk, I had to take whatever edge I could get.

Christian stood on a ladder, hammering a nail into a 4x4. His eyes lit up when they landed on Angelica. We needed to talk fast because I knew Christian would be heading to baseball practice soon. I was still reeling from my earlier exchange with Ang and her insinuations about my feelings for Kyle, so I was happy to use the case as a distraction. I decided to channel all the nervous energy and dive right into the deep end.

"Hey, Christian, what's up?" I said, looking up at him.

Christian glanced at me before his eyes went right back to Angelica.

"Hey there, Angelica, what brings you down here?" he said, grinning at her.

"That's a great question," she said under her breath. I discretely elbowed her.

"Huh?" Christian grunted as he stepped down the ladder, still ignoring my presence.

"I was in the neighborhood. Just stopped by to see how the sets were going."

"You're in the production?" He smiled. "In that case, we better make the sets extra nice. I had no idea you were interested in musical theater," he said, never taking his eyes off her.

"I have many interests you don't know about," Ang replied with a breathy voice.

"Oh? I'd be interested in learning about all of them." Christian grinned so wide it looked like it hurt.

"I just bet you would," Angelica said, raising one corner of her lips.

Excellent! Now that she'd put him at ease, it was my turn.

"Hey, Christian, I just wanted to congratulate you on all the wins with the baseball team. I hear you and Andy have been killing it lately." I was taking Big Momma's advice and laying it on thick.

Christian finally turned and glared at me. "What are you talking about, dipwad?" That was a better reception than I had expected. At least he hadn't called me Sissy Sinclair.

"How would you know? You suddenly a baseball fan?" Christian raised his eyebrows and cocked his head to one side. "Shouldn't you go make like a nerd and put your head in some book?"

There it was, the attitude I had been waiting for. Angelica stepped closer to him. "Is that any way to treat an adoring fan?" she said more calmly than I expected.

"Oh, sorry," Christian said, his tone softening.

"Evan is here on official school newspaper business," she stated before twisting her head and winking at me.

It took me a second to get where she was going before it hit me like a lightning bat. "Yes, I've become quite a fan. I just interviewed Coach Bennett for a story I'm doing on the team." Well, it was sort of true. There was no story, but I had interviewed him.

"Is that why you've been hanging with that douche, Jayden? I've seen you all over his jock lately." Christian rolled his eyes.

My shoulders stiffened. Angelica looked down at the floor. It almost looked like she was trying not to laugh. Was that really what people thought? My face flushed. I shrugged, trying to remain loose and casual, but my insides were screaming. My hands began to shake. "Naw, it's not like that. I had to get some quotes from him for the article."

Christian's face lit up. "Oh, so are you here to get some quotes from me?"

I hadn't thought about that angle, but Ang decided to go with it. "Of course, he is. Why else would he be here?"

I followed her down the rabbit hole. "You're the new star player now that Jayden has lost his lightning bat."

Christian curled his lip. "Yeah, what a shame. I guess his Thor bat wasn't so lucky for him after all."

"I know. Poor baby. He's still groaning about it." I was all in.

"He just needs to get over it."

"For real." I saw my opening. "I wonder who could've taken it."

"Who cares? The bat's worthless. It wasn't forged by the gods like all those morons think. He needs to find another bat and come down out of the clouds."

"He's got a point," Angelica chimed in as she looked at me and smiled.

I glared at Angelica before turning back to Christian. "Well, it definitely worked out for you. Some people might think you nicked it." I smirked, watching for Christian's reaction.

Christian's jaw tightened. "Who said that? Did somebody on the team say that?"

"A few might have mentioned it."

"Are you serious? I had nothing to do with that. They're just throwing shade." Christian scowled. "Like I care enough about some phony lightning bat to take it."

"You were at practice the day it went missing." I was going in for the kill, but I noticed Ang discreetly patting her hand down, indicating for me to "slow my roll," as she often said.

"Yeah, so were a lot of guys. Anyways, I had a doctor's appointment that day and had to leave early. So I wasn't even there when it all went down. I was long gone."

"Oh?" That wasn't what Kyle had said.

"Yeah, my shoulder's been messed up, probably from swinging that thing so much," he gestured to the hammer on the ladder beside him, "so the coach told me to get it checked out."

"Poor baby," Angelica said, which knowing her was meant to be sarcastic, but it was lost on Christian, who looked at her and smiled.

"Can anyone verify that?" Now, I sounded like a detective.

Christian's jaw clenched as he stepped closer to me. "Are you saying you don't believe me, Sissy Sinclair?"

There was the Christian I knew. I didn't have time to answer before his face was only inches away from mine, exhaling his peanut butter breath right on my nose. Things had gone pear-shaped.

"Sounds like mister gay boy here is calling me a liar," he said while poking his finger into my chest.

"No, that wasn't what I was saying," I replied while taking a step back.

"No wonder my dad says all you gays should burn in hell."

Ang attempted to step between us. "Christian, take it easy, geez."

Christian sideswiped her, getting so close to me I could see the pulsating veins in his neck. "You think I took that fake magic bat, don't you?"

"No, no . . ." My heart was pounding. The last thing I wanted was to ruffle Christian's feathers. I wouldn't stand a chance. I took another step back, once again attempting to put some distance between us, but my foot met an apple box, sending me flying backward. Everything went dark for a fraction of a second before I realized I was lying flat on my back and staring up at the ceiling.

CHAPTER 9

THE PINCH HITTER

I held the ice pack up to my head and winced as it sent shivers down the back of my legs. I sat in the nurse's office looking up at Principal Albert, who was nervously running his fingers through his short, disheveled brown hair.

"I'm OK. Really." I'd been saying the same thing for the last few minutes, ever since Mr. Ferguson, the shop teacher, had forced me to come here.

"Are you sure?" Principal Albert looked from me to Christian, who stood silently, for a change, on the other side of the room. "So tell me again how this happened." Principal Albert was wearing a wrinkled beige suit that was slightly too tight for his short and stocky build.

"It wasn't my fault. He just fell," Christian said, finally breaking his silence and giving me a secret look that said I better keep my mouth shut.

"So you two weren't fighting?" Principal Albert asked, looking me square in the eye. I could hear the skepticism in his voice. I could only imagine how many times he had to question Christian on these types of skirmishes. Christian had a reputation for having a violent streak. Looking back, I realized I should've given that more consideration before I questioned him.

I finally spoke up, "No, we were just talking, and then I tripped on something behind me." I left out the parts where he had nudged me with his finger and had gotten up in my face. There was no need to place a bigger target on my back. I was already mortified. This was certainly not going to help me rise to popularity.

"See, I told you," Christian said, validated.

"Alright, alright. I just had to be sure." Principal Albert turned from me to Christian. "Especially when you're involved, Mr. Carlson."

I almost laughed but thought better of it at this particular time.

"So can I go now? I'm missing practice," Christian said, scooting toward the door.

"Yes, you're excused, Christian. Just *please* stay out of trouble."

Christian bolted from the room without looking back. I tried to get to my feet. "I better get going too." I needed to get to Big Momma's and tell her what I'd uncovered.

"And just where do you think you're going, Mr. Sinclair?" Principal Albert softly put his hand on my shoulder, guiding me back into a sitting position. "I've notified your grandmother, and she's on her way to pick you up."

"You called Big Momma?" I did need to talk to her, but not like this.

He nodded, shouting over his shoulder as he walked across the hall to his office. "She should be here any second. So put the ice pack back on your head, sit back and relax until she gets here."

I groaned. I was never going to live this down. I could see the social media headlines already: *Christian lands Sissy Sinclair in the Nurse's Office.* I leaned back and did as the principal had instructed, this time the ice sending chills down the front of my arms.

After what seemed like an eternity, I finally heard Big Momma's voice out in the main office in the same corridor but just to the left of the nurse's office. She and the school's office assistant, Mrs. Powell, had been going to church together for years, so I hoped they wouldn't get into one of their long gossip sessions. Then it hit me. This time, that might work in my favor.

Big Momma hurried into the office. She was wearing a bright green dress that brought out the hazel tint of her eyes. It was odd not seeing her in one of her exotic caftans. "Evan, are you OK?" She leaned over me and placed her hand on my head as if she was looking for proof that I was hurt.

"Yes, I'm fine." I pulled back. "I don't know why they called you."

Big Momma stood upright. "Well, they tried that dad of yours first, but of course, he was in a meeting and couldn't be disturbed. Good thing you weren't seriously hurt."

Principal Albert walked by and stuck his head in the room. "Good to see you, Ruth. Thankfully, he isn't too banged up. Kids these days. Never a dull moment," he said, laughing.

"Isn't that the truth? Thanks for calling me. I'm going to get him home." Big Momma took the ice pack and set it down on the desk beside her.

Principal Albert grabbed it. "I'll take care of that. I don't believe he suffered a concussion, but you might want to get him checked out anyway."

"I'm fine. I just hit my head." I waited for Principal Albert to retreat down the hall before I motioned for Big Momma to stoop down so I could tell her what I needed her to do.

"What is it, dear?" she said, bending over.

"I talked to Christian today, and he said he had a doctor's appointment the day the bat went missing. Can you find a way to confirm that with Mrs. Powell? I don't believe a word that knob says."

"Evan, I don't know. Should you be worried about the case right now? Your health is more important than a baseball bat."

"I'm fine." I was getting so tired of saying that, but Big Momma's eyes were heavy upon me. I knew she wasn't convinced. "Honestly." I gave her my best puppy-dog eyes.

"OK, but I want to hear every detail of this incident when we get home."

"I promise." I raised my hand in a three-finger salute.

Her eyes softened. "And just how am I supposed to do this, Mr. Smarty-pants?"

"I don't know, but you always think of something." Big Momma always said that flattery got you everywhere.

"This is true. Give me a minute." She placed her finger on her chin and sat down on the chair across from me. "What is the boy's name again? And which day was it?"

"Christian Carlson and the bat was last seen on Monday."

"I'll be right back." Big Momma stood up and made her way into the office.

I jumped up and stood just inside the door where I could poke my head out and witness the exchange.

"Hey, Sister Powell, can you do me a favor?" Big Momma wasted no time as she leaned on the front counter.

Mrs. Powell stood up from behind her desk and walked over to the counter. She was a larger woman. The other kids called her fat, but she was what Big Momma would call big-boned. She was the only African-American staff member who worked in the school's office. "Of course, Sister Anderson, what do you need?"

"That Christian Carlson boy, do you know if he was at school last Monday?" Big Momma inquired.

"I'm not sure. I could look it up, but we usually don't give out that information." She lowered her voice. "Does this have something to do with Evan?"

Big Momma lowered her voice to a whisper. "Yes, it does. Monday, Evan came home with a bruise on his face. He said he fell off his bike, but now after this incident, I'm beginning to think this Christian kid might be bullying him. Of course, he denies it, but I'm worried sick, and I just need to be sure."

Wow, Big Momma was good. Miss Marple had nothing on her. My legs were getting tired as I shifted my weight from one foot to the other while still trying to remain out of sight.

"Poor Evan! Just between you and me, it wouldn't surprise me if it was Christian. He's always in here for fighting. His parents need to do something with him." She slid over to the computer sitting on the left side of the counter and pushed a few buttons on the keyboard. "It looks like Christian was here on Monday but only until lunchtime. He was signed out for a doctor's appointment that was scheduled for 2:00 p.m."

Christian had been telling the truth. He had been at a doctor's appointment that afternoon. Although, as a detective, I had to think about every possibility. Christian only lived a few blocks from the school, so he could have easily come back after seeing the doctor and stolen Thor. It was a bit of a stretch, but I wasn't taking him off the suspect list just yet.

"So it could have been him. I think I'm going to need to have a talk with his parents. Thanks so much, girl. I owe you one."

"Don't mention it. I wanna keep Evan safe just as much as you do." She smiled and walked back to her desk.

A sweaty hand clutched my shoulder. "Whatcha doing, Evan? You feeling better?"

I gasped, almost jumping out of my skin as if I had been caught taking the last slice of pizza before everyone else had had some. I flipped around to see Principal Albert staring down at me. "Um . . . yeah . . ."

Big Momma, hearing me, raised her voice. "Evan, you ready to go?"

I exhaled with relief. "Yes, Ma'am." I shuffled out of the nurse's office and down the hallway to the main office.

"Take care, Evan. Good seeing you again, Ruth," Principal Albert called out as Big Momma and I exited through the main door.

Down the hallway, once we were out of earshot, Big Momma said, "Word of advice, Evan, if you want to be a detective, you're going to have to be a much better spy."

CHAPTER 10

THE SLIDER

Big Momma and I were just about to exit the school when I realized I'd forgotten my algebra book in my locker. I grunted. It was going to be quite a challenge to complete my homework without it. "I forgot my algebra book. I'll meet you at the car," I blurted over my shoulder as I whirled around and raced down the hall. "Meet me at the side door." That entrance was much closer to my locker.

With school being over, the hallways were practically empty, with only a few stragglers leaving their club meetings, so I was able to dart through the school and retrieve the book in record time. As I was exiting the building, I heard a loud whack. I scurried toward the noise to see a boy sprawled out on the sidewalk with a skateboard on top of him. Seeing his curly black hair, olive skin, and familiar bright emerald eyes. I immediately knew it was my former bestie, Patrick Hendricks.

I looked down at my injured friend. "Patrick, you okay?"

All I could hear were Patrick's moans under the board. "Evan?"

"Yeah, Pat, it's me. You OK?"

I wasn't at all surprised he was riding a skateboard. I'd occasionally see Patrick in the caf hanging with his new skater friends. He stuck out being the only Latino in the bunch. Patrick never had an issue going against the grain, not that I could talk, being black, and loving country music. Being the only two brown boys in cub scouts led us to become fast friends.

"I'm fine, just clumsy." Patrick's face was beet red.

As I was lifting his board off him, I saw that not only had Patrick slimmed significantly from our grammar school days, but now small muscles rippled down his arms and legs. Must have been all the skateboarding. The jock kids could certainly no longer tease him the way they had in elementary school by calling him "Fatrick."

"Are you sure? You're bleeding." I looked away, feeling light-headed after glimpsing his open scrapes and the blood running down his right arm and left leg.

Patrick, suddenly remembering, said, "Oh, sorry, *amigo*. I know how you are about blood."

If anyone knew, it was Patrick. We had been inseparable in elementary school. I'll never forget the day during fifth-grade recess when the class bully had pushed me down the slide, flinging me into the pointy steel corner. Blood had gushed everywhere. I stood up, saw it, and immediately passed out. Patrick had taken me to the nurse's office, and I'd ended up getting seven stitches.

"It's okay. You could say I owe you one." I smiled and looked into his eyes. Patrick smiled back, welcoming my gaze.

"Nah, you don't owe me anything. That's what *amigos* do."

A knot grew in the pit of my stomach, and I knew exactly why. Patrick had lived only two houses down from me. Then his parents had divorced, and he had moved a few blocks over with his mom, landing him at a different elementary school. Both of our elementary schools fed into Lincoln, putting us at the school again, but I would only say "hi" and "bye" to him and rush off whenever he came around so nobody would see us together.

Lincoln was supposed to be a new start for me. I wanted to shed my nerdy, sissy image. Both Patrick and I had been relentlessly teased for being girly and told we were gay. My offense had been having a high-pitched voice while Patrick's had been being too good of a gymnast. Not to mention, we had both hung out with all the girls during lunch rather than playing sports with the boys. So, in their minds, as Big Momma put it, we had been ripe for the picking.

Then last year, after losing Mom, my school status had been the last thing on my mind. Ironically, Patrick had found his own flock with the skaters, and I had been the odd man out, eating lunch every day by myself in the lunchroom or library until I'd met Angelica. That was why it was imperative I got in with the untouchables now while I was still in middle school because everyone knew that once you started high school, it was almost impossible to switch tribes.

Patrick plucked at his sleeve, which was sticky with blood from his skinned arm.

Seeing his cut, I winced as if I was the one bleeding. "Maybe you need to stick with biking instead of skateboarding."

"Haha," he said, wobbling his head from side to side.

Big Momma pulled up beside us in her SUV and rolled down the window. "Well, look who it is . . ."

She stopped abruptly when she noticed the blood on his arm and shorts and exclaimed, "What in the world happened?"

I spoke for him. "Patrick had an unfortunate altercation with the curb."

"You poor thing. Get in the car. We're going to get you cleaned up."

"Hola, Big Momma," he said, limping toward the car. I couldn't help but smile. Patrick was probably my oldest friend. We'd begun having sleepovers at Big Momma's when we were six years old, so if anyone could call her Big Momma, it was Patrick.

Patrick steadied himself against the SUV. "That's not a bad idea. If my mom sees me like this, she will freak out. She's still not sold on the whole skateboarding thing."

Would she ever! Patrick's mom was a huge worrywart. She would take his board away in a heartbeat. When we had been kids, and I'd hang out at his house, she wouldn't let us play with Legos because she was afraid we would choke on them.

I empathized with Patrick's plight, but I was still apprehensive about his coming to Big Momma's. I was finally squeezing my way in with the popular kids, and the last thing I wanted was Patrick jeopardizing that. Yes, he hung with the skater tribe now, but if people, namely the bros, saw us together again, it would only be a matter of time before the homo wisecracks would start up all over again.

I sighed, seeing the blood running down his arm, I said, "Well, you're pretty gross with all that blood."

"Gee, gracias," Patrick laughed as he flung his arm in the air, causing blood droplets to hit the sidewalk like a crimson mist.

"Pat! Ugh . . . Gross." I leaned down and picked up his board, carefully avoiding his blood splatter. I looked around and didn't notice anyone watching us. "Get in the car. I'll put your board in the back." I figured Big Momma could patch him up quickly, and then he could be on his way before anyone saw us together.

CHAPTER 11

THE CLEANUP

I could tell Patrick was in more pain than he was letting on by the way he limped through Big Momma's front door and bit his upper lip with each excruciating step. Patrick's face didn't relax until he got a whiff of her signature coffee aroma, which filled the air.

"Gosh, that coffee smells good," Patrick said, now seeming less concerned with his wounds and more interested in getting a cup of the coffee. Back when he and I'd been inseparable, Patrick had come over all the time to have coffee with me and Big Momma.

Big Momma had hustled into the house before us and had just returned from the bathroom with supplies. "Well, don't just stand there, Evan. Get him a cup. What have I told you about your manners?"

I blushed. "Yes, Big Momma, I was just about to ask him if he wanted a cuppa."

She squinted at me as I dashed into the kitchen to hurriedly grab Patrick's coffee. I had to make sure Big Momma cleaned Patrick up quickly and sent him on his way before he ruined everything.

Patrick laughed. "I guess Evan still loves his British shows."

"Are you kidding? He never misses them. He even has me watching them," Big Momma said as she started to tend to Patrick's wounds before yelling toward the kitchen, "Oh, and Evan, please text your father. I have two missed calls from him. I'm sure he's looking for you. He's working my last nerve."

Yours and mine too, I wanted to say but thought better of it. With all the commotion, I had forgotten to text him again. I knew this wasn't going to go well. I retrieved my phone and sent him a message.

Sorry. At Big Momma's now. Had to help a friend who crashed on his skateboard.

I didn't want to go into any more detail. That should be enough for him to see there were extenuating circumstances.

I poured Patrick a cup of coffee and returned to the living room. It must have taken longer than I thought because Big Momma already had his arm cleaned and bandaged. "Took you long enough." She smiled, and Patrick couldn't help but laugh.

I handed him the cup, and he took a sip. "Be careful; it's hot," Big Momma warned.

Patrick didn't seem fazed at all. "No, it's perfect. It's just as delicious as I remember."

"Aw, aren't you sweet . . . See, Evan, you should bring Patrick over more often. It's been way too long."

Don't go giving him any ideas. I fidgeted with my fingers and looked down at the numerous coffee stains on the mustard yellow shag rug. Big Momma had a soft spot for Patrick. When we'd stopped hanging out, she'd constantly asked me why. She'd told me I'd better be careful because I was getting too big for my britches when I told her I'd outgrown Patrick and wanted to make new friends.

Like Angelica, Big Momma didn't understand why it was so important for me to join the untouchables. Why couldn't they see that having the untouchables' validation would be a game-changer for me? If they accepted me, everyone in the school would finally see that I was just like everyone else, rather than the nerdy, gay-acting black kid who didn't fit in anywhere.

My phone beeped.

We are going to have a serious talk when I get home tonight.

I rolled my eyes, shoving my phone back into my pocket. *Joy. I can't wait.*

"I take it he's not happy," Big Momma said, seeing my face.

"Nope, not at all," I said, looking up at the ceiling. "He wants to chat when he gets home tonight."

"And who knows what time that will even be," Big Momma sneered.

Patrick looked at us with a confused look. I shook my head. "Trust me; you don't want to know." Nor did I want him to know that my dad was tracking my every move.

After two more cups of coffee, Patrick was sitting in the rocking chair next to Big Momma, laughing, talking, and feeling right at home. Big Momma grinned. "So, do you still watch that *Avatar* show?"

Patrick smiled sheepishly. "I'm more into skateboarding now than *Avatar*."

"Well, I sure hope you get better at it," Big Momma said, looking at his bruises.

They both laughed as I shifted my weight from one foot to the other. This had gone on long enough. Patrick was stitched up and all better. It was time for him to go.

"Patrick, you better get going. It's getting late. I'm sure your mom's looking for you. You know how she is."

Big Momma turned toward me, narrowing her eyes. "Evan, don't be rude!"

Patrick tried to stifle a laugh. "He's probably right. She's been known to freak out."

I glanced at him, unamused. I knew he was referring to when Patrick didn't call her when we had an impromptu ice cream outing after our weekly cub scout meeting, and the police showed up at the Braum's Ice Cream Shoppe. In her defense, earlier that week, a few kids at our elementary school had been relentlessly calling him a wetback, so her guard was already up. I'd forgotten that in addition to being called gay, he had to deal with those racial slurs as well.

Big Momma looked at the clock over the stove. "Oh my, it is getting kinda late. Patrick, why don't I drive you home? It's getting dark out."

"No, I'm fine, Big Momma, and it's just two blocks up the road. But I better get going; tonight is tamale night."

My tummy rumbled at the mention of Patrick's mom's cooking. All of her dishes were delicious. Being invited to his family dinners was definitely something I missed by no longer hanging out with him.

"Okay, then you better get going now while there's still light out. Evan, walk him to the door." She shot me a quick you-better-do-what-I-say look. "It was great seeing you again, Patrick," she said, reaching out and hugging him. "Don't be a stranger. Even if you don't stop by to see Evan, you can always stop by and see me and have some coffee." She smirked, knowing it would irk me.

As I walked Patrick to the door, he stopped and turned to me. "I forgot to ask, were you in detention or something this afternoon? Why were you around so late to catch my wicked spill?" Patrick asked with a slight grin.

"Detention? Really?" I couldn't believe Patrick would think that I was in detention. I stuck out my chest. "Actually, I was working a case."

"A case? Like a detective or something?"

I remained silent.

"Does this have anything to do with why you were hanging with Kyle in the caf yesterday?"

My eyes lit up. Dang, word was getting around. "Nosy much?"

"I keep an eye on my mates, even old ones."

I almost smiled but thought better of it. I didn't want to give him the impression that I wanted to be friends again.

"You aren't the only one who watches *Masterpiece Mystery* every Saturday night," Patrick teased.

I wasn't at all surprised. Patrick had always loved mysteries just as much as I did. "Well, if you must know, I'm looking for Jayden's missing bat."

"That thunder bat or whatever they call it?"

"Thor." I could barely maintain a straight face as I said it. "I heard Jayden talking about it going missing at lunch the other day, and I decided to help him out . . ." And just like that, against my better judgment, I told him the entire story, including my interrogations of Kyle, Lammy, and Coach Bennett and my altercation with Christian. It felt like old times confiding in him. Plus, unlike Big Momma, it was nice to talk to someone who was actually familiar with everyone involved.

"WHAT?" Patrick shouted so loud I had to take a step back. "You ended up in the nurse's office?" He shook his head. "Christian is a total *pendejo*. You better watch your back."

"I'm good," I said, more to assure myself than Patrick.

Patrick grabbed his skateboard out of Big Momma's SUV and started up the street before turning around.

"Hey, E . . ."

He caught me just before I closed the door. "Uh, yeah," I swallowed hard and stuck my head back out, hoping he didn't want to discuss why we weren't friends anymore.

"You need some help figuring out what happened? I wouldn't mind being Dr. Watson to your Holmes." He looked down at the pavement.

I chortled. "You mean more like Nancy Drew to the Hardy Boys."

Patrick looked up. "Hey, she solves mysteries all on her own."

"Thanks for the offer, but I'm good," I said, avoiding his gaze. Now I regretted having told Patrick everything. Maybe one day we could be friends again, but not now. I was too close to my goal.

His face dropped. "Kk, I better get going."

Hearing the disappointment in his voice, my stomach twinged, but I ignored it. I had to focus on solving the case and upping my social status. That was all that mattered. The last thing I wanted was Patrick mucking it up.

Patrick smiled. "BTW, he'd be lucky to have you as an *amigo*. I know I was." He jumped on his board and glided down the driveway.

As I closed the door, the stomach tingle returned.

CHAPTER 12

THE ANGEL IN THE OUTFIELD

"So, what was this fight about?" Standing at 6'2", my dad was looming over me like Optimus Prime, only he was dressed in a gray Italian suit with a purple shirt. Dad loved purple, and it was a great contrast to his dark complexion. His hair was thinning on top, which is why he kept it cut short.

He hadn't stopped yelling since Big Momma had brought me home, and I had planted myself on the living room couch. He finally took a breath. "Did you at least win?"

"It wasn't a fight, Stephen." Big Momma was standing near the front door. "They were talking, and Evan tripped and fell back and hit his head." I was sure she was planning her escape at any moment. She hadn't even taken her bright yellow shawl off. I was surprised she had lasted this long in the same room with my dad. The two of them usually avoided each other because, when they collided, it was like adding gasoline to a flame.

Big Momma leaned against the door frame. "And you know Evan's not a fighter. He's way too sensitive to engage in such undignified activities."

Dad scowled. "Don't remind me!" Dad furiously paced up and down the living room. I was surprised he hadn't burrowed a hole down into the center of the earth.

Big Momma sucked her bottom lip. I knew she was trying to stop herself from saying something inappropriate. She finally spoke. "You're making way too much out of this. It was an accident. How about you support him rather than berate him?"

Dad glared at Big Momma. "Now you're telling me how to raise my son."

"Hmm . . . How's that going for you? He's at my house more than he is here. Maybe you need to think about why that is." Big Momma didn't stop herself this time.

Dad frowned and then took a long, deep breath. "You may not agree with my methods, but I'm doing the best I can." Dad folded his arms. "It's not just about today's fight. He's not texting me immediately when he gets to your house after school." He looked at me. "Isn't that right, Evan? I haven't forgotten about that. I don't know what is going on with you."

"The texting is a bit much . . ." Big Momma said.

"And what exactly is wrong with wanting to know where my kid is?"

My foot tapped feverishly as I watched them rehash the same arguments they'd had for the past year– ever since Mom died.

I finally just leaned back on the couch and contemplated any other possible leads I might have overlooked in the case. Jayden was definitely going to ask for an update when I saw him at the library tomorrow. That is *if* he showed up.

I finally heard Big Momma say, "We aren't solving anything here, and I need to get going. I don't like driving at night."

Dad looked as if he had moderately calmed down. His face had softened, and he wasn't breathing as heavily as he had been before. "I'll walk you out."

"No need," Big Momma said without missing a beat.

My dad didn't miss one either. "I insist," he said as he rolled his eyes and then focused them on me. "*You* get upstairs and start studying your books of the Bible. Don't forget we have a BTU competition on Sunday."

Oh drat, I had forgotten all about that. I detested Baptist Training Union. I jumped off the couch and kissed Big Momma on the cheek. "See you later, Big Momma. Thanks for coming to get me." I turned and darted up the stairs, hearing the front door shut behind me.

I opened the door to my room and plopped my book bag down on the bed. I flopped down beside it. I wanted to ask Dad if I could skip the BTU, bible competitions thing and just go to church with Big Momma after I got back from the library — she would probably be picking me up anyway — but I already knew his answer, especially if it involved going to Big Momma's Seventh-Day Adventist church. A resounding "*No!*"

Being the son of a Baptist pastor, Dad had gone to church every Sunday and attended all the services, including BTU, so he expected no less from me. Baptist church services offered me nothing but incessant boredom. For a while, I'd tried sneaking comic books inside the hymnals, which I pretended to peruse during the sermon—anything to keep me awake and divert my attention from Pastor Franklin's scornful sermons. Unfortunately, Dad had caught me one Sunday when he'd inadvertently knocked the hymnal out of my hand, thus exposing the comic. Dad's lips had pursed so tightly together that I could see the muscles in his jaw tightening.

Now we didn't leave the house Sunday morning without Dad giving me a pat-down, like a petty thief, to ensure I didn't have any literary contraband. The only thing I was permitted to have in my possession was my cell phone, and that was because I'd told him I used the Bible app to follow along with the scriptures during the sermon. Little did he know I had also downloaded the Kindle app and had access to hundreds, if not thousands, of books.

Dad had once asked me how I could love books and not at all be interested in "the Good Book," which was what he called the Bible. I didn't dare tell him I had read many more interesting books.

Reluctantly, I stood up and pulled that so-called good book down off my overly packed bookcase. I fell back onto the bed and tried unsuccessfully to imprint the books of the New Testament back into my memory. I'd memorized them many times before for previous competitions, but I couldn't concentrate. My brain kept going back to my conversation with Angelica. How long had she thought I was gay? And how did she figure out that I was starting to fancy Kyle? But what startled me the most was that she hadn't ridiculed me. She acted as if my being gay didn't matter. I squinted, trying to remember if anyone had ever told me that just being me was OK. Certainly not Dad.

Suddenly, like a sharp sting across my face, I saw my mother in the hospital bed, barely recognizable after months of chemotherapy and radiation, which had rendered her down to the meager figure that lay in front of me. Every time I'd looked at her that way, I'd wished for the vivacious mother I'd known before ovarian cancer had overtaken her body. On that last day, she'd called me over to her bedside. She'd smiled and said, "Hey slugger, what have you done to your hair?"

I used the tips of my fingers to pat down my unruly locks. Mom had always said I'd gotten them from her father, Big Daddy. "Nothing," I whispered, moving closer to her.

"I can see that." She reached for my hand, pulling me beside her. "How about you put a brush through it?" She giggled.

There she was. That was the spunky Mom I knew. She was still in there.

I clasped her limp, cold hand. I shuddered with fear as she began having one of her coughing fits, allowing me to see the outline of just about every bone in her body. Feeling like I wanted to flee, but at the same time not wanting to leave her side, I grasped her hand even tighter as I leaned over her.

After the coughing subsided, she looked directly into my eyes. "E, I want you to promise me something."

I cleared my throat, trying to dislodge the lump deep inside. I tried to find my voice but instead choked on the tears that were now streaming down my face as I gently placed my head on her chest. I sobbed uncontrollably, feeling the skin stretched tight over hard bone. I wished for the softness I remembered, longing to be held in her arms like a little boy one last time.

"It's okay, my beautiful boy. You have such a huge heart. I love you so much." Her cold, fragile hand brushed against my wet cheek. "I remember when you were a baby. You could sit for hours and just entertain yourself. You didn't even need a toy. You were curious about everything, your feet, your hands, your clothes, your blankets, your stuffed animals. You were always trying to figure everything out. You were always so happy." She placed her other hand on mine. "Don't ever let anyone take away your spirit. You're gonna be an amazing man, and everything about you is perfect."

I sniveled, trying to clear all the mucus trapped in my nose while inhaling the pungent disinfectant aroma that filled the hospital room.

"I knew how special and different you were even before you were born." She smiled, making my chest hurt more. "I have always known. You're my perfect little man," she said, her voice sounding like the familiar, firm voice I had always known. And that was when she said it. "I love you unconditionally, and that will never change, no matter what. I will always be with you." She tightly grabbed my hand. "I will always be smiling down on you."

The machines suddenly let out a chorus of beeps. A nurse rushed in, checked the monitors, and leaned her hand on the call button. "Code blue in room 113," she said. "We need you out of the way," she shouted as she almost shoved me out of the room. Dad, who had been waiting outside, grabbed my shoulders, pulling me out of the way of the doctor in a white coat who was rushing into Mom's room. Then he went into her room with the others, leaving me alone. I stood outside, trying to peer through the windows, but I could only see a crowd of indistinguishable bodies crowded over her. A few minutes later, Dad opened the door; his face drenched with tears, he stooped down next to me and whispered, "Evan, Mom's gone. She's up in heaven with the angels."

I sat upright on my bed, wiping the tears from my face. I'd give anything to hug her one more time. She'd have known what to say. I could always just be who I was with her. I needed her right now more than ever.

CHAPTER 13

THE CUTOFF MAN

I checked my phone again for what seemed like the hundredth time. 9:14 a.m. Still too early to call Jayden. I'd first awoken at 7 a.m. I'd kept tossing and turning, hoping I would fall back asleep, but who was I kidding? I was way too excited. I got out of bed and paced around the room. I had to find something to do to keep myself occupied until it was time. My pulse quickened like I was doing one of my cross-country runs. I'd never gotten this nervous when I was hanging out with my old elementary friends, but this was more than that. This was Jayden Stevens and Kyle Reynolds, the ultimate BMOCs. I had to make this library day epic. I had to show them that despite being a brainiac, I was still an awesome, normal dude so that once I found the bat, they wouldn't have any doubts about welcoming me into their fold; everything depended on it.

I ran downstairs and scarfed down a bowl of cereal. As I shoveled the sugared flakes into my mouth, I looked around the kitchen, spotting Mom's archaic-looking black and white mixer. Dad had always threatened to buy her a new one, but she'd always refused, saying she had gotten that mixer as a wedding present, and from the very first time she had used it, it had been enchanted with a special magic, which is why everything she made with it tasted so good. Now that I thought about it, that must be how Jayden felt about Thor.

I threw my bowl in the sink and ran back upstairs to check my phone. 9:26 a.m. *Still too early to call.* I opened my closet to pick out what I was going to wear. I pulled out a few of my most colorful polos – a blue, red, yellow, and green one. I decided on the bright blue one. My gut fluttered when I realized it would match Kyle's eyes perfectly. As I was putting the other polos back in the closet, I heard my phone chime. My heart pounded like I'd been shot with adrenaline. It had to be Jayden. He was up and ready to go.

"Hello," I bellowed into the phone as I plopped onto the bed.

"Hey, E. It's Patrick. You're cheery for nine in the morning."

My heart sank to my feet. "Uh . . . yeah." I cleared my throat. "What's up?" *Why was he calling?*

"So . . . I'm gonna help you solve the case," Patrick said very matter-of-factly.

I sighed. "Listen, Pat, I told you I have it covered."

"I know that's what you said, but you and I both know you need my help."

I remained silent.

Patrick was not giving up. "C'mon, for old times' sake. How many mysteries did we watch with your mom, and we practically solved them all? Together, we'll figure out who took the bat in no time."

He did have a point. We were pretty great when we worked together. When we had been in fourth grade, we had created a jazz band, with Patrick playing the saxophone and me on the piano. It had been short-lived, but we had won the talent show. And no one could beat us when we'd teamed up to play Trivial Pursuit when Coach Tidwell had preferred to chat on his phone during class rather than teach us social studies. I had to admit I really could use some of that teamwork right now. I had a few leads, but nothing concrete. And it's not like anyone had to know we were working together.

"Okay, fine, but we have to keep this low-key."

"Kk, if that's how you want it." I heard disappointment in his voice. My gut wrenched. I didn't want to hurt Patrick, but I was finally infiltrating the untouchables, and I couldn't let anything, or anyone jeopardize that, not even him.

He must have been reading my mind. "Those so-called untouchables don't deserve your help. You're way too good for them."

I snorted. Where had I heard that before?

Then in true Patrick-style, he bounced right back. "So, do you have a prime suspect?"

"My gut's telling me that Christian and the coach are hiding something. I'm just not sure what. The coach also claims he wasn't around when the bat was stolen."

Patrick laughed. "Was he at the doctor's too?"

"No," I couldn't help but chuckle. "Supposedly, he coaches a Little League team and was on his way there when the bat was stolen."

"Little League team?" Patrick's voice rose an octave. "Do you know which one?"

"No, I didn't ask. Is that important?"

"It could be." Patrick paused.

I racked my brain trying to figure out which clue Patrick saw that I didn't.

"I have an idea. I'll do some checking and get back to you. Thanks for the update. It's going to be fun working together again."

"Hey, wait a minute. Patrick . . . Patrick . . . Patrick."

The phone clicked. What was he up to? I was just about to call him back and demand an explanation when I heard the familiar creak of my door opening up farther. If Mom were still alive, she would've already had the WD-40 in hand and applied it generously on the door. She hated such irritating noises.

I looked up to see Dad dressed in another one of his three-piece suits, standing in the doorway and scowling down at his phone. He was probably already late for a meeting.

"Dad, you scared the crap out of me." I sat upright on the bed as I hung up the phone.

"I heard you say, Patrick. Was that your old friend Patrick from Elwood?"

Elwood was our old elementary school. "Yep." I didn't elaborate.

"So, you're talking to him again. I thought you guys fell out."

I looked at the floor, letting out a faint grunt. He barely communicated with me other than surveillance texts and telling me when to be ready for church. He was usually too consumed with work to even notice me. Now all of a sudden, he wanted to know about my life.

"Fell out?"

"Got mad at one another," he clarified.

"I wasn't mad at him. He moved away, and we just went our separate ways." That wasn't exactly the truth, but I didn't want to recap all the unpleasant details, not with him.

"I'm glad you guys are talking again. I always liked him. He's a good kid." That was interesting. He usually didn't like any of my friends, not that I had many to pick from.

I hastily grabbed my backpack and began removing my books. I wasn't used to having such deep conversations with Dad. Normally, "how are you" and "how's your day" were as heartfelt as our conversations got.

"I also heard you say something about Little League. Are you thinking about playing baseball again? Going to all those games with your mom must have rubbed off on you."

There was that optimism in his voice. Ever since I could walk, he'd enrolled me in various sports, hoping I'd have some innate ability for one of them, but much to his chagrin, I was terrible at just about all of them. At least Mom had just been happy with my being a spectator when I accompanied her to the Ranger games.

"No, Dad, I'm helping a friend find his lost baseball bat."

"You're helping him find a baseball bat?" Dad scoffed. "How did you get roped into that?"

"I offered. It's no big deal." I didn't want to talk to him about this. Dad had been a star basketball player in school, so he had no idea what it was like not to be popular.

"Can't he just use another one?"

Really, Dad? I took a deep breath before responding. "It's his lucky bat. He's been on a winning streak ever since he's had it."

"Wait a minute. Does that have anything to do with that scuffle you had with that kid at school?"

"Sorta." My stomach twitched. I could already feel where this was going.

"Did you accuse him of taking the bat? Is that why he pushed you down?"

"He didn't push me down. I tripped," I said, trying not to raise my voice.

"Are you sure you want to get involved in this bat thing? Look at the trouble it's already gotten you into." He jerked his head to the side. "This kid you're helping, is he white?"

This again. "Yes. Why does that matter?"

"It doesn't," he said, trying to deflect, but I knew better.

"Would you be OK with my helping him if he were black?"

"No, I'm not saying that. But it wouldn't hurt for you to have at least a few friends of color, like Patrick. Friends who can relate to your specific experiences."

No wonder he was so happy about my talking to Patrick again. "My friends are my friends. It doesn't matter what color they are."

"In this world, it matters. You'll always be seen as a black man, and that's something your white friends will never understand."

I got his point, but I didn't appreciate the way he was making it. He was belittling me and my choice of friends. I guess they weren't good enough for him either, except for maybe Patrick.

He leaned against the doorframe, his face softened. "I'm just looking out for you, son. The rules are different for those who look like we do. Why don't you hang out with some of the kids from church?"

I rolled my eyes. "Because they hate me."

"They don't hate you. You just haven't given them a chance."

I looked down at the carpet. "They certainly don't miss a chance to call me names." I could feel his eyes on me.

"What are they calling you?"

Oh no, there was no way I was telling him that. I was uncomfortable enough having this conversation with him. I certainly wasn't opening *that* can of worms.

"It doesn't matter." I finally looked up at him. "Dad, I'm just helping a friend find his bat, isn't that the Christian thing to do?"

His lips pressed tight, and I could see the disappointment in his eyes. "Of course, it is, but sleuthing is not something you can put on a college application. They're going to want to see you're well-rounded, with real extracurriculars like playing a sport and being involved in church." He walked toward the bed. "I want you to be able to attend the university of your choice."

Yeah, right. He's always using college as an excuse, but I knew what he was really saying. "Well-rounded" was code for a "real man." In his mind, it was fine for me to be a good student as long as I walked the straight and narrow, went to church, played sports, and proved that I wasn't "soft." Just like the kids at school, he was calling me a sissy.

"I get that you're helping a friend, and that's great and all, but just make sure that it doesn't distract you from your studies." His eyes narrowed. "And I need you to do a much better job of keeping me informed of your whereabouts. I'm not trying to control your life, but as your parent, I need to know where you are for your own safety. If you can't follow the rules, I won't hesitate to take your phone and require you to come home every day and call me from the landline so I can be certain you're here, which would mean not going to Big Momma's. Are we clear?"

I looked up. "Yes, sir." My blood was on fire. He wanted me to be more pious, more black, more athletic. I was never good enough in his eyes. And he wondered why I'd rather hang out at Big Momma's. At that moment, I couldn't help but feel that cancer had taken the wrong parent. Then I immediately regretted the thought.

"I'm taking off. Are you going to the library?"

"Yes. I guess you're working today." He was always at work, so why should today be any different?

"Yeah, I have a few things I need to catch up on."

"Big Momma's taking me, so I'm sure she can pick me up." I needed him off my back, so I could continue the investigation.

"I'll be downtown so *I* can pick you up. I don't want you there all day. You need to get back and continue working on your BTU drills." His voice became an octave deeper.

I started to protest, telling him that I could study at the library, but decided it was just easier to comply. "Yes, sir." Besides, I didn't believe him for a second. Once he got engrossed in work, pulling him away was like ripping chewing gum out of hair. I was counting on him working all day because I'd told Kyle and Jayden we'd go ice-skating after hanging in the library.

"I gotta run. Text me when you're done." Dad disappeared down the hallway.

I reached for my phone. 10:00 a.m. on the dot. It was time for the moment of truth. I'd planned to get there at noon, so I figured two hours would give Jayden and Kyle enough time to get themselves together and meet me there. I licked my lips, then opened my mouth as wide as I could before exaggeratingly twisting my lips from side to side and then in all directions. I caught my reflection doing this in my dresser mirror and laughed out loud. You would think I was auditioning for the lead role in a play. I was just asking Jayden to join me at the library. And he'd told me to call.

I picked up my phone, my hand shaking as I steadied myself to dial the number. The phone rang four times, and just when I was expecting it to go to voicemail, Jayden picked up. There was a lot of clatter on the other end. It sounded like Jayden's phone had hit the floor and got shuffled around before he could retrieve it. I finally heard a muffled "What's up?"

"Hey, Jayden," I said a bit loudly. I thumped my head. That sounded way too perky, considering Jayden sounded like he had just rolled out of bed. "It's Evan. You told me to call if I was going to the library today. I'm getting there around noon if you and Kyle are still up for hanging out."

"Oh, yeah . . ." Jayden said softly in a half-asleep, raspy voice. Immediately, my heart sank. In his current state of disarray, I expected Jayden to say to forget it, but to my surprise, he cleared his throat and said, "We'll be there. See ya around noon."

I almost yelped before pressing my hand against my chest, my fingers splaying out, and then taking a deep breath. "Okay, great. Text me when you get there."

I threw the phone down and jumped onto the bed, bouncing up and down. I was going to the library with Jayden and Kyle. This was a dream come true, but now the pressure was on. I had to make sure they had a good time, so they'd come with me every weekend. Everything was falling into place.

CHAPTER 14

THE SHUTOUT

"Are you meeting Patrick?" Big Momma asked as we climbed into her SUV.

"No, Patrick and I aren't friends anymore. I was just helping him because of the accident. I have new friends now."

Big Momma raised an eyebrow. "Oh, is that so, Mr. Top Dog? And just who are these new friends?"

"Jayden and Kyle. You don't know them." I didn't want to go into more detail for fear of having to answer all kinds of questions about them, such as who their parents were, where they lived, where they went to church, etc. "I'm meeting them at noon."

"Isn't Jayden the one you're helping find that supposed magic bat?"

"Yes, and Kyle's his best friend." I was hoping she would leave it there, but I knew better.

Big Momma curled her bottom lip. "And they both just decided to hang out with you at the library all of a sudden?"

"Yeah, we've been hanging out lately. They've been totally cool."

"Yes, because they want something from you. I wouldn't trust them as far as I could throw them."

"They're coming to hang with me at the library today. They wouldn't do that if they weren't my friends."

She rolled her eyes. "Suit yourself. You're gonna have to learn the hard way."

I tuned her out. It was pointless to argue with Big Momma. I knew she was coming from a place of concern, but I was going to prove her wrong. Jayden and Kyle were my friends now.

I pulled out my phone to see if there was a message from Kyle or Jayden. Nothing. I clicked on my playlist, put in my earbuds, and cranked up the Lady A song playing. I decided to send Angelica a text.

Guess who's hanging with me at the library today? 😊.

I couldn't wait to rub her nose in it because she had been so sure they wouldn't come.

When she stopped the car at the curb in front of the white-brick building, Big Momma asked, "Do you need me to stay just in case they don't show up?"

"No, they're coming," I said, not sure who I was trying to convince more, her or myself. I still hadn't gotten a text from Jayden or Kyle saying they were on their way, which was a bit concerning.

"I hope so, but call me if you need me to fetch you."

"Dad's at work. He said he'd pick me up."

"Of course he is. Where else would he be?" she mumbled under her breath. Big Momma wasn't shy about commenting on how much Dad worked. Being a financial consultant was demanding, so I understood why he had to work long hours, but I'd hoped after Mom died, things would change. Instead, he worked even longer hours than before.

"Thanks, Big Momma. Love you." I jumped out of the car. It was already 12:15.

The Fort Worth downtown library took up an entire city block. The enormous, ten-story building had just been renovated two years earlier. I entered through the gigantic double doors at the main entrance and walked onto the second floor, past the checkout desk that occupied most of the room. Just behind it, a set of stairs led down to the first floor, the reference floor. It seemed natural to head down there after coming through the main entrance, especially for those who weren't familiar with the layout, so I figured that's where Kyle and Jayden would go first.

I reached the bottom of the stairs and looked around the reference section. No sign of them. Maybe they already found their way to the fifth floor. That was the multimedia floor with all the music, movies, and the theater room where they held seminars and children's storytime. I had loved story time as a child. Mom had first started bringing me when I was six. It had been another one of our special places. The books would come alive right in front of my eyes. The puppet shows had been our favorite, encouraging us to clap and sing along.

The elevator opened to the fifth floor, and I hurried to the movies section. The library had hundreds of titles of movies, old and new, on DVD. While I preferred streaming movies on my phone or iPad, these were all free, and more importantly, here, I could watch practically anything I wanted rather than viewing it at home under my dad's discerning eye. Sometimes I just picked a title at random and watched the first five minutes of it. If I wasn't hooked, I would pick another.

I'd watched an intriguing movie during my last visit based on a play that had been turned into a movie back in the '80s. The lead character was gay, dressed up in women's clothes, and had an irritating, raspy voice. He was looking for love and acceptance, and neither came easy, especially from his disapproving mother. He had undergone terrible heartaches and tragedies, including his cheating lover, who died after being gay-bashed. But somehow, the lead character got through it and eventually had a very fulfilling life. According to Dad and Pastor Franklin, that wasn't the normal fate of gays and lesbians. Maybe they'd been interacting with the wrong gays and lesbians.

I strolled through the maze of cubicles. Each one was equipped with CD/Blu-Ray players and monitors so patrons could watch a film or listen to one of the thousands of CDs or vinyl albums if they could nab one of the few cubicles with an old-fashioned record player. There were only two of them, and they were always in high demand. I had been lucky enough to have claimed them a few times. I loved listening to Ravel's *Bolero*. I remembered it from the cartoons I'd watched as a kid, but listening to the album version made it come to life.

As I rounded the cubicles, I came to the shelves that housed all the DVDs. There were at least twenty shelves with about a hundred titles on each side. According to one of the librarians, they had the largest selection of titles of all the libraries in the state of Texas, except for the Lyndon B. Johnson Presidential Library in Austin.

I finally saw Jayden and Kyle in the middle of the shelves, looking through the action section. Jayden turned to see me. "Evan, this place is lit." Jayden was beaming. "They have everything."

I hadn't seen him that happy in a while, at least not since his bat had been stolen.

Jayden grabbed another DVD off the shelf, his hands full of movies blustering with gunfire and bullet holes. "They have the entire series, even the ones my mom won't let me watch," he said, still grinning from ear to ear.

Kyle nodded in agreement. "Who knew? You nerds do know where to find the good stuff." His head titled in my direction. "It is pretty sweet."

"I told you guys. I wouldn't lead you astray." I wasn't quite sure what that meant, but Dad always told me that when I was resisting trying new food only to discover it was delicious.

Jayden smiled and patted me on my shoulder. I decided to take another chance. "Hey, we should post a pic."

Jayden looked around the room. "At the library?" he said with a confused look.

"Why? Are you afraid it'll ruin your reputation?" Kyle laughed. "Or that people will realize that you actually know how to read?"

Jayden tapped Kyle on the back of the head. "Shut up." He looked back at me and smiled. "Sure, why not? I'm going to tell everyone how cool this place is anyway. And I might score some points with Kushaela." He put his hand up to his chin. "She likes smart guys."

My head jerked back. I had no idea Jayden liked Kushaela. But she was the head cheerleader and the school's resident queen bee, so together, they would make the quintessential power couple. Although, I'd always assumed Kyle and Kushaela had something going on because they were joined at the hip.

Kyle snorted. "Give it up, Jay. You don't have a chance."

I tried to control my excitement as I retrieved my phone from my pocket. "Okay, let's take it over here in front of the DVDs."

Jayden moved over to my right side while Kyle slid behind us, sandwiching himself between us and wrapping his arms around each of our shoulders. Kyle placed his chin on my shoulder. A shiver shot down my spine, making me even more nervous as I held the camera out in front of me and snapped the picture.

"You gonna post it?" Jayden asked, digging out his phone.

"Yeah, I will." *Are you kidding me? I'm hanging out with two of the most popular kids at school in the library, of all places. There's no way I'm not posting it on SnapBabble.*

"I don't think you're my friend on SnapBabble. I'll send you a request," Jayden said, still looking at his phone.

"Uh . . . I don't think I am either. I will too." Kyle was also now captivated by his phone.

"Okay, sounds good." I tried to play it cool, but my inner voice shrieked with excitement. OMG, I was now friends with Kyle and Jayden on SnapBabble. Wait until I tell Angelica. She will flip out.

Jayden's eyes suddenly grew wider. "What?! Evan! Christian landed you in the nurse's office?"

My heart fell into my gut. Crikey! I had forgotten all about that. I started to explain, "No . . . well, yeah . . ."

Kyle looked up from his phone. "I just saw it too. What the heck happened, E? It's all over SnapBabble."

This was exactly why I hated SnapBabble. I should have known all the trolls on there would be having a field day with my latest demeaning debacle. "It was an accident . . . We were talking, and I fell." My face grew hot as my brow started to glisten.

"You were asking him about the bat, weren't you?" Jayden was almost jumping up and down. "I knew it. He took it, didn't he?"

Kyle arched his eyebrows. "Did Christian take it?"

"No, it wasn't Christian," I said, slightly raising my voice. "He had a doctor's appointment the day it went missing, so he wasn't even at practice." I looked around, making sure none of the librarians were headed our way to quiet us down.

"You sure?" Jayden scratched his jaw. "I could have sworn I saw him by the lockers."

"I even double-checked it with the office." I was going to tell him that I still had my doubts about Christian's story, but I thought better of it. The last thing I wanted was to incite a repeat of the Jayden-Christian confrontation I'd witnessed the other day in the cafeteria.

"So, who took it? I thought for sure it was him," Jayden said, sounding defeated.

"I have some other leads I'm following up on. Just give me until Monday."

Jayden ground his teeth. "The championship game is Wednesday. That's cutting it close."

Kyle, obviously sensing Jayden's frustration, tapped him on his arm. "E's on the case. He'll find it. He's too big of a nerd not to." Kyle winked at me and laughed.

"True. True," Jayden said with a slight smile. "OK, I'm gonna go watch this. You guys comin'?" Jayden put his phone away and headed to the cubicles.

"I'll be right there. Save me a spot next to you. I'm gonna pick something out," Kyle said as he sprinted over to the science fiction section.

"I'm gonna grab something too. I'll meet you guys over there." I knew what I wanted to watch, and today was the perfect day to watch it. I walked over to the comedy section, and luckily, it was available.

Everything was going right for a change. I smiled to myself. It was about time I finally got some wins.

CHAPTER 15

THE DOUBLE PLAY

Jayden had the headphones around his ears and was already engrossed in the bullet-riddled film. Kyle stood in the next cube stuffing his DVD into the player. It was *Star Trek: Into Darkness.* I smiled. Good choice. I loved *Star Trek,* especially the movies with Chris Pine. He played Captain Kirk perfectly. His charisma drew me in, much in the way Zac Efron's did. That's saying a lot because I was *so* not a musical fan, but I had seen all the *High School Musicals* multiple times, primarily because of Zac. Patrick and I had watched each one at least twenty times back when we were besties.

"No way! Is that what you're watching?" I boomeranged back to reality to find Kyle standing next to me, looking down at my popular teen comedy movie.

"Yeah! I've seen it so many times, but I love it."

"Me too."

"*Star Trek* is a good choice too. I really like Chris Pine."

"He killed it."

I grinned as I entered the cube beside Kyle. Who would have thought Kyle and I would have so much in common?

"Although, Zachary Quinto is my favorite. He's a great Spock." Kyle quickly glanced around before whispering, "Do you know he's gay in real life?"

Taken aback, my face boiled like it was going to burst into flames. "Oh . . . really . . . I think I remember hearing that." I knew this for a fact because I couldn't read enough about his coming out via social media a few years back.

"You'd never guess, right?" Kyle winked. "Okay, well, I'm gonna seek out new life and new civilizations, to boldly go where no one has gone before."

We both laughed as Kyle sat down and turned his attention to the screen.

I took a seat in my cube, still unsure of what had just happened. I had to text Angelica. I grabbed my phone and saw she had responded to my earlier message.

How much u wanna bet they don't show up? Pics or it didn't happen. :-)

I texted her back.

You'd lose. Hahaha! They're here. We're watching movies.

I attached the picture we all took earlier.

I opened SnapBabble on my phone to find both Jayden's and Kyle's friend requests. I accepted them and then posted the pic, tagging them both and writing the caption: *"Saturday at the library with the peeps LB."*

I wanted to get as many "likes" as possible and hopefully counter all the current gossip about my squabble with Christian. Despite my disdain for social media sites, there was no way I wasn't going to include a picture of me hanging out with two of the most popular kids at school. Surely with them in the picture, I wouldn't get the normal barrage of hateful responses I usually received from my classmates when I posted something.

I was just about to hit play on the DVD player when my phone chimed. Angelica texted.

OMG! I just saw ur post.

I texted her back.

Ye of little faith.

That was another phrase I had stolen from Big Momma.

I continued the message.

We're besties now. :-)

Angelica responded immediately.

You wish! SMH. How are things with ur bf Kyle? :- (kissy face)*

I rolled my eyes as I poked at my phone.

Shut up. 😊 *But he said something kinda strange.*

Jayden snickered loudly, causing me to jump. I looked over to see him engrossed in some comical part of the film. Kyle noticed too, and just turned to me and laughed.

My phone chimed again.

I told u. He's a hot pot of mess! What did he say?
I texted back.
I can't get into it now, but I'll call u later tonight.
 I couldn't wait to fill her in. I knew she would give me her honest opinion without any sugarcoating. She replied.
U better.
I placed my phone on the counter, hit play on the DVD player, and sat back to enjoy my movie. I had seen it dozens of times, but it was especially appropriate today of all days because it focused on a female protagonist, Stacy — who was at the top of the high school social pecking order — befriending two less popular kids, allowing them to hang with her friends, which ultimately leads them to become more popular than even she was. It was the Cinderella story of school popularity.
I desperately needed a Stacy to take me under her wing. Angelica was awesome, but she was no Stacy. But thanks to my current arrangement with Jayden, I was finally on the fast track to becoming an A-lister. I was particularly fascinated by one of the popular wannabes in the film, who wasn't initially open about his sexuality, but by the end of the film came out, and everyone accepted him for who he was. More importantly, he ended up becoming part of the "IT" group. That always gave me hope, which is probably why I watched the film so often.
When the movie ended, I looked over my cube to see the black screen staring back at Kyle as he played Candy Crush on his phone. Jayden was still feverishly engrossed in his movie.
Kyle looked up. "He just started the second one. He's gonna be at it all day," he said with a half-grin. "I wanted to check out some sci-fi or fantasy books."
"You like those too?" I bounced up onto the tip of my toes with excitement. "I can show you where they are. It's on the third floor."
Kyle tapped Jayden on the shoulder after he and I put our movies back on the shelves and were ready to head downstairs.
"Have fun. You know where to find me," Jayden yelled way too loudly, thanks to the headphones he was wearing, before getting back to his action flick.

We took the stairs down to the third floor and headed straight to the science fiction section along the back wall. I was like a kid in a candy store, as Big Momma would say. Kyle and I searched through the various titles lining the shelves.

"Have you read *A Wrinkle in Time*?" I asked, skipping down the aisle, still not believing I was at the library with Kyle Reynolds.

"Of course, I loved it."

"Really? It's one of my favorites. What about the *Chronicles of Narnia*?"

"Yep, I read them all."

"No way! What about the Darkover series?"

"Duh . . . Darkover is fierce."

"Yeah, it is." My mouth hurt from grinning.

"Have you read her other book, *The Catch Trap*?"

"No, just the ones in the series."

"You mean there is a book you haven't read. Can't be." Kyle teased.

I looked over at him and smiled.

"It's not a sci-fi book, but you'd like it." Kyle turned toward the shelf, stooped down, and scanned for the title. I joined him, seeing the authors' names all ended in A, so we had to go down two shelves before finding the B's.

"Dang it, it's not here," Kyle huffed.

"Are you sure it's the same author?" I asked.

"Yeah, but it's not science fiction, so I'm thinking, that's why it's not here."

"Oh, it's not." So why did Kyle think I would like this book? But hey, Kyle Reynolds suggested a book for me to read, so I was just going to go with it. "We can always ask a librarian. I know most of them anyway." I quickly realized that didn't make me sound cool.

Kyle laughed. "Of course you do. You take being a nerd very seriously."

"Hey, even you said there's more to do here than you thought," I said.

"On the real, it's pretty cool. I wish I'd known. I'd have come sooner." He patted me lightly on the shoulder. It startled me at first, but then I relaxed and smiled, feeling a strange sensation. I was chuffed, as they said in the British mysteries. I truly couldn't remember the last time I had been this elated, at least not since Mom had died.

We walked up to the help desk, but there was no librarian in sight. Kyle stood next to me, biting his nails. I could tell he was getting impatient, so I slipped behind the desk and typed the title into the search screen. I was a pro at using the library database.

The title popped up on the screen. "They do have it. It's in the historical fiction section" I wrinkled my nose. "That sounds like a book my dad would read." I turned back to Kyle, still wondering why he thought this book would interest me.

"That's it. It's set in the '50s or something."

I scrunched my forehead, still not convinced.

Kyle winked. "Trust me, E. You'll like it. I know you will."

There he went, calling me E again, causing my face to glow. "Okay, if you say so." I jotted down the call number before we trotted to a section of the library I'd never been in before, and that was saying something, considering I had been up and down most areas of the fiction floor.

Once we found the correct shelf, I verified the call number and retrieved a large, hardback book that looked as thick as a spellbook from a Harry Potter film. It must have been close to 800 pages.

"Wow, you didn't tell me it was an epic saga."

"Yeah, it's a long one, but it goes fast. A big nerd like you, you'll be done in no time," Kyle snickered. "We should probably start working on that paper."

Oh, crap, I'd forgotten all about that paper. "Yeah, you're right."

I led Kyle over to a table in the center of the room, and we sat down and got to work on his *Romeo and Juliet* paper. To my astonishment, he'd read the play, making it fairly easy to help him outline the three major themes — love, conflict, and family. I helped him organize his thoughts and even gave him a few ideas for how to start each section.

It seemed like it'd only been thirty minutes when Kyle looked at his phone. "Oh, geez, it's almost been two hours. I bet Jayden is looking everywhere for us."

Kyle and I raced to the elevator. As we stepped inside, I realized that I didn't want my time alone with Kyle to end.

"Hey, have you been up to the rooftop lounge?"

"Dude, this is my first time ever stepping foot in this library," he laughed. "But you had me at rooftop. Let's go!"

CHAPTER 16

CLIMBING THE LADDER

I pushed the tenth-floor button. The doors closed, and Kyle asked, "So where exactly are we going?"

I looked around the elevator nervously. "I don't want to ruin the surprise."

"So, do you take all the library newbies up here?"

I blushed yet again, confused as to why he kept having that effect on me. "Not all of them."

We exited the elevator and made our way up the steps to the roof-top access door. Kyle looked around the desolate floor. The corridor did look like the setting of a horror film. It was kinda cute seeing Kyle getting anxious. "You sure we're allowed up here?"

"Oh yeah. It's a secret hideaway that only we regulars know about." Finally, I sounded like a cool library nerd.

I opened the door, and Kyle's mouth flew open. Swanky leather lounge chairs and love seats nestled between planters with huge palm tree–looking plants. There was a large white bar in the center of the room with about twelve white leather barstools around it. The rooftop lounge was enclosed in glass so you could look right up into the sky, and with the sun almost setting, it was a beautiful sight.

"Welcome to the rooftop lounge," I said, knowing this would win me major points.

"This place is fire. You can see all of Sundance Square." Kyle said, running up to the edge of the glass enclosure. "How do you know about it?"

"I've been up here tons of times with my dad for his business stuff." Dad was always winning awards for something — National Association of Black Accountants, YMCA Chairman's Award, United Negro College Fund Award; you name it. They all usually included a small reception on the rooftop.

"Lucky you." Kyle walked around the bar area.

I didn't always feel lucky when it came to attending Dad's events. Yet, it was one of the few things we actually did together. I was lucky to know about this place, and it had become my hideaway when no functions were going on.

"The only other person I ever brought up here is my old friend Patrick."

Kyle's head popped up from behind the bar. "Not Fatrick Hendricks?"

Uh-oh, I should have kept my big mouth shut. "Yeah, we kinda hung out in elementary school."

"You used to hang out with that gay skater-punk *cholo*? Really?" Kyle erupted with laughter. "He's such a loser. I'm glad you have better taste in friends now." Kyle steered toward the love seats.

I bit my tongue. I might not be friends with Patrick anymore, but he wasn't a loser and, he certainly didn't deserve to be called a *cholo*, even jokingly. I opened my mouth to protest, but the last thing I wanted to do was ruin my budding friendship with Kyle, so I changed the subject. "C'mon, let's look around."

After sitting in all the chairs and love seats and checking out all the snacks at the bar, which unfortunately were under lock and key, we settled down on the love seat and gazed at the setting sun.

After a few minutes of contemplation, Kyle broke the silence.

"Thanks for your help with the paper." Kyle's eyes darted from side to side. "I've wanted to talk to you about something."

I gulped, the hairs on the back of my neck now at full attention. "Oh?"

"So what's the deal with you and that wiggy red-haired girl you're with all the time?"

I hid my grimace. Angelica hated it when people called her that. "Angelica? She's quickly becoming my BFF."

"Cool, I kinda figured that."

I wasn't sure how to take that comment. His phone chimed. He fished it out of his pocket and glanced down at it. "It's just Kushaela."

My eyebrows rose. "Is she gagging for you?"

"Uh . . . what?" Kyle said with a blank look on his face.

"Really into you?" Truth be told, I wasn't exactly sure what it meant, but when the characters on the TV shows were said to be doing this, they were head-over-heels infatuated with someone. "They say it all the time on my PBS murder mysteries."

Kyle laughed. "You know, for a brainiac, you're kinda funny. And it's so not like that with Kushaela. She's my ride-or-die."

"That's good because it sounds like Jayden has a thing for her."

"Jay getting with Kushaela will never happen," Kyle said. "She's totes out of his league."

I sat back on the love seat, feeling secure in the fact that Kyle was starting to consider me a friend.

We sat in silence for a few more minutes before Kyle broke it again.

"So, what's going on with the case? Any other leads so far?"

"I've kinda hit a wall right now. Coach Bennett and Christian were my biggest leads, and they both seem to have alibis."

"I thought for sure it was Christian," Kyle said.

"Yeah, me too, but he probably has the most reliable alibi, being at the doctor and all. The same can't be said for Coach Bennett."

Kyle's jaw snapped shut. "Huh?" He bolted upright. "I doubt the coach had anything to do with it. Don't you have any other suspects?"

"Well, technically, everyone at the practice that afternoon is a suspect. They all had means and opportunity." I sat up tall, proud to be sounding like a real detective.

"Even me?"

I laughed. "Well, of course not you. He's your best friend," Kyle's eyes seemed brighter in the twilight. I found myself not being able to look away.

"True that," Kyle said, breaking eye contact.

I looked down at the sofa and tried to bring my focus back to the case. "Now I'm just trying to figure out who else might benefit from the bat's disappearance," I said, finally getting my thoughts back on track.

"You have any ideas?"

"Yes, I do." Truth was, I didn't, but I had to appear competent if I wanted them to believe I could find the bat before the big game. "I need to do more digging before I make any accusations. I don't want Jayden going off half-cocked."

His eyes grew distant as his face hardened. "Oh, yeah, he can be savage. I know that better than anyone." Now that's a surprise. I had always thought Jayden and Kyle were the best of friends, but, of course, best friends could grow apart. Look at what had happened to me and Patrick.

Kyle's eyes brightened. "Did you ever talk to Lammy? What did he have to say for himself?"

"He admitted to being in the locker room after practice when the bat was taken, but he's the one who told me that Coach Bennett was hanging about acting suspiciously."

"Did he also tell you what he and Jayden had gotten into it the day before?"

My head jerked back. "No, he didn't. He conveniently left that part out."

Kyle grinned. "I bet he did."

"Do you know what the disagreement was about?"

"No idea. I just heard him clap back at Jayden, telling him that he was an arrogant jerk and that he would be nothing without that bat, which has kinda proven to be true," Kyle said with a smirk.

I couldn't tell if he was serious or his typical sarcastic self, but I was more concerned with why Lammy hadn't told me about the squabble. "I think I better have another chat with Lammy. Thanks for the tip."

"Like I said, I'm happy to help." He sat back and folded his arms against his chest. "This whole thing is driving Jayden crazy. Today has been a good distraction for him. Good looking out." He grinned and placed his hand on my back.

A shudder shot through my body. I enjoyed talking to Kyle, especially when it was just the two of us. When we were alone together, Kyle acted like a completely different person, a stark contrast to our previous interactions.

Kyle's smile faded. "While we're talking about possible suspects, you do know about the bet between Jayden and Andy?"

"Andy Falkner?" I scoffed. I'd considered Andy as a suspect, but I'd dismissed the notion because I knew he was friends with Kyle and Jayden and a fellow untouchable. But thinking back, I did recall Jayden saying something about a bet he made with Andy the day I was eavesdropping on them in the cafeteria.

"Yeah, Andy bet Jayden at the beginning of the season that he could hit more home runs than him. It's a lot easier to win that bet when someone doesn't have their lucky bat." Kyle leaned closer to me, prompting my toes to tingle. "And he was at practice the day the bat went missing, and now that Jayden sucks, he's getting all the attention."

My eyes bulged. "Isn't he one of you and Jayden's BFFs? Do you think he is capable of doing something so despicable to Jayden?"

Kyle smiled. "As you said, everyone's a suspect."

He did have a point. I made a mental note to chat with Andy. Based on this new information, he could have taken Thor to ensure he won the bet. And even if he hadn't, since he had been at practice the day it had gone missing, he could have seen something that could lead me to the culprit. And just like that, I had two new suspects. Maybe I really could get this case solved by the championship game, all thanks to Kyle.

Kyle's phone beeped repeatedly. He looked down at the screen.

"You're blowing up, Mr. Popular," I said.

Kyle sniggered. "You're getting me mixed up with Jayden. Everyone loves him," he said, raising his hands and looking up to the sky. "He's the golden boy who can do no wrong."

Again, I wasn't sure if Kyle's tone was one of mockery, resentment, or both.

He looked back at his phone. "It's the picture you posted of the three of us that's getting all the attention. We already have over 275 likes."

No way! I couldn't help but smile. Whenever I normally made a post, it would maybe get 100 likes, and that was after a week, not a couple of hours. It paid to be SnapBabble friends with the BMOCs.

I slapped my knees. It was getting late, and I still wanted to take them over to the mall to get ice cream and ice-skate. I had to give them the full library experience, Evan-style. "We better go pry Jayden away from the movie so we can head over to the center."

"Lead the way!"

We jumped off the love seat and ran toward the elevators.

CHAPTER 17

THE SEVENTH-INNING STRETCH

Kyle and I returned to the fifth floor, where we found Jayden in the same cubicle, engrossed in the third *Transporter* movie. After some serious persuasion, we pulled him away from the monitor. I guided them down to the basement to the secret corridor that went underground to the Saeller Center across the street. It really wasn't a secret. It was just that very few people used it, so it was usually deserted. It was just a boring, white cement underground walkway secured by an automatic double glass door. When I was younger, it had been the only way my parents would allow me to leave the library on my own, so I had taken it out of necessity, but now it was just fun. Kyle and Jayden found it fascinating.

"I feel like I'm in Harry Potter," Jayden said.

Kyle was right. It was good to see Jayden having fun and not worrying about his bat for a change.

"I do feel like I need a wand in here," Kyle laughed, waving his arm in the air like he was casting a spell. He stopped and raised one arm in the air. "Expelliarmus."

All three of us broke out in rambunctious laughter. Fortunately, we were the only ones in the tunnel.

Our first stop had to be Bahama Buck's. Kyle and Jayden must have thought so, too, because they immediately began hooting and hollering with excitement as soon as we emerged from the tunnel and saw the sign.

Every time my mom would bring me to the library, we always stopped at BBs. Her regular order had been a strawberry-banana-coconut-flavored snow cone. I decided to get that exact same one in her honor. Kyle ordered a strawberry cream snow cone, and Jayden went tropical with banana-peach-mango.

We walked toward the ice-skating rink, which was right smack in the middle of the six-story center, so no matter which floor you were on, you could look over the railing and witness all the hijinks on the ice. We aimlessly walked toward the rink, sticking out our tongues and comparing the colors created by the snow cones. Mine was a deep purple, while Kyle's was bright pink, and Jayden's had a yellow-orange tint, like the color of a beautiful sunset.

We somehow ended up at the second-floor railing, where we stood finishing our snow cones as we looked down at the twenty or so skaters circling the ice rink. I couldn't wait until it was our turn to take a few spins or spills around the ice. I wasn't the best ice skater, but I could at least skate around the rink without having to grip the side barriers, which I noticed a few people doing as I looked down at the skaters. I could even manage to skate backward and do a couple of turns. I was hoping that would be enough to impress Kyle and Jayden, especially since this was one of the few athletic activities at which I didn't completely suck.

Jayden and Kyle were almost finished with their snow cones, staring intently at the rink, when a teenage girl, fifteen or sixteen years old, attempted a layback spin only to find herself belly up on the ice. Jayden and Kyle both erupted in laughter. "Now, that was an epic fail," Jayden said in between snorts.

Kyle sagged against the railing, choking with laughter. "OMG, did you see her face? Classic. She was like . . ." He broke off, unable to speak, and flapped his hands to express himself.

"Harsh, that looks like it hurts." I tried my best not to laugh, but I didn't win the battle. Besides, I didn't want to seem like a prude in front of Jayden and Kyle.

The girl gathered herself up, allowing the boys to get a better look at her lanky frame and notice the stray strands of strawberry blonde hair sticking out of her ponytail. Jayden's jaw almost hit the floor. "Wow, she's straight fire."

"Yeah, she is." Kyle looked her up and down before jabbing Jayden with his elbow. "Why don't you go see if she is okay?"

"I just might."

"I dare you."

"You wanna bet?"

"I'll give you ten bucks."

"Done!" Jayden ran over to the railing just above the girl, waving his hands to get her attention.

I watched in amazement as the girl smiled up at Jayden from the railing below. They were soon engaged in conversation, but it was too far to make out what they were saying. I wish I had that much confidence.

"Damn, looks like I'm out ten bucks." Kyle moved closer to me, brushing up against my arm. "Hey, E, check out those two guys." Kyle pointed to the other side of the rink where two guys in their mid-twenties were laughing and hanging onto each other as they precariously skated down the rink.

I laughed, thinking Kyle was poking fun at their obvious poor ice-skating skills.

"Do you think they're gay?" Kyle looked me right in the eyes.

I wasn't sure what to say. "Um . . . I don't . . . Why would you say that?"

"They are all over each other."

"I think they're just trying not to fall." I didn't know why I was trying to defend them. I didn't even know them, but I knew better than anyone how much it hurt to be made fun of for being gay, and I didn't want to be a part of that.

"Maybe, or they could just be really into each other." Kyle winked.

"I guess . . ." I couldn't tell if he was making fun of them or not. What was it with Kyle today? This was the second reference he had made to someone being gay. I was so accustomed to being assaulted with gay references that I couldn't distinguish when someone was disparaging and when they were genuinely supportive.

I looked over at Jayden, who was still chatting it up with his new ice-skating friend. Hopefully, he would come back soon. I enjoyed my alone time with Kyle, but all this talk about gay stuff was kinda weirding me out.

"What's wrong?" Kyle touched my arm again. "Don't you think two guys can get together?"

"Yeah, of course, I just . . ." I couldn't find the words. Kyle moved closer, slightly leaning up against me.

Kyle tightened his grip, "I believe you have to be open to everything."

"That's not what my pastor says . . ."

"Screw those religious fanatics. They're such hypocrites. God wants us to be happy, and if being with another guy makes you happy, I say go for it." His lips now inches from my ear. "Don't you?"

Before I could answer, a phone chimed behind us. Kyle jerked back and quickly released my arm as we turned around to see Jayden waving his phone in front of him. "Who's the man?"

"No way, you got her number?" Kyle grabbed for the phone.

"Was there any doubt? And I want my ten bucks." He lightly punched Kyle on his arm.

My phone vibrated in my back pocket. I pulled it out to see a text message from Dad.

Leaving now. Be there in 10 min.

No, not yet. My fingers frantically glided across my phone as I texted back.

I'm still working on stuff. I won't be done for another 30 minutes.

Figures, the one time I had wanted him to get buried in work so he would be running late like usual was the one time he was done early. We hadn't even gone ice-skating yet.

After a few seconds, my phone chimed with his response.

You've been there long enough. You have 15 minutes. See you outside.

Crud! I had to find a way to ward him off. The question was, how?

CHAPTER 18

TAKEOUT SLIDE

I grabbed my ice skates off the counter and hurried to an empty seat beside Jayden and Kyle, who were already lacing up their skates. I didn't want to rush ice-skating, but I also wasn't sure how long I could keep Dad at bay, especially since he was so adamant about picking me up. I couldn't help but wonder why all of a sudden, that was so important to him. It must have to do with that ridiculous BTU competition. Dad was super competitive about everything, so I didn't know why it surprised me. Lord forbid I embarrassed him by forgetting one of the books of the Bible.

I racked my brain, trying to think of a way to get him to allow me to stay longer. He was ruining everything. *I got it.* I stopped lacing and retrieved my phone.

Book checkout line super long, I don't want u to have to wait. Big Momma can pick me up. See you at home.

There, that should do it.

"C'mon, Evan, what's taking you so long?" Jayden stood up, wobbling on his skates. "I'm ready to get out there."

"You sure about that?" Kyle rose next to him, catching Jayden's arm to throw off his balance. "You're looking pretty shaky to me."

"Hey! Let go!" Jayden freed himself from Kyle's grasp. "Let's see who falls first."

"Well, we already know who that is going to be." Kyle looked down at me as I frantically tied the final knot on my skates. "Don't we, E?" They both laughed.

"Don't be so sure," I said, standing up, trying desperately to maintain my balance as I hurled myself toward the entry to the rink. *I will show them.*

I carefully stepped out onto the ice. The last thing I wanted to do was fall as soon as I entered the rink. I would never live that down.

My blades touched down on the ice, and I put my hand on the wall just long enough to get my bearings before I pushed myself off and torpedoed myself into the crowd. I dodged the other skaters and slowly started making strides to increase my speed. By the time I reached the other end of the rink, I was relatively secure on the skates, so I sped up, feeling invigorated as the breeze hit my face.

"Look at E go," I heard Kyle say, quick on my heels. "Wow, you can skate. Who would have thought?"

"Yeah, not bad, Evan." Jayden was now approaching me on the left.

I decided to change it up. I held my breath as I flipped around and started skating backward. I shocked myself at how easily I crushed it without the hint of a stumble.

"That's on fleek," Jayden said. "Show me how to do that."

I beamed. I couldn't believe my ears. Jayden Stevens just asked *me* to show *him* how to do something?

Kyle put some pep in his step as he frantically attempted to catch up to me. As he came closer, he held my gaze, his blue eyes sparkling like sapphires. It was like he was coming right for me. I wanted to look away but couldn't. He skated toward me until he was only a few inches from me, still looking directly into my eyes. I bit my lip and struggled to keep my balance, hoping I wasn't going to run into anyone behind me. Just when I thought he was going to reach out and grab me, he winked and then flipped around and began skating backward alongside me on my left.

He smirked at Jayden. "You mean you can't do this, Jay?" He chuckled. "Poor baby."

Jayden frowned. "I hate you both."

I saw my opening. "It's easy. I can teach you."

"Really?" Jayden perked up.

I decided to take it up another notch. "I can teach you this too." I looked behind me and glided into the center of the rink, where I pivoted onto one leg, raising the other one straight out in front of me, and did a double twirl. It took me a second to come to a complete stop, but fortunately, I was able to use my toe pick to suspend the momentum while lowering my other leg back onto the ice, maintaining my balance. To borrow Angelica's saying, *I Slayed!* I struck a pose by leaning back and flashing the backward V sign in front of my chest like I was posing for a photo.

"That's fire," Jayden said, skating his way over to me and patting me on the back.

Those ice hockey lessons had paid off. That had been my dad's bright idea back when I was in sixth grade. Much to my dad's chagrin, I'd never become a good player, but I did excel at the ice-skating component.

Kyle skated up behind Jayden. "Who knew dweebs could be such good ice skaters?"

Jayden whacked him on the back of his head. "You're just mad because he's better than you."

"Oh yeah, I forgot, no one is better than you at anything," Kyle said, not at all hiding the sarcasm in his voice.

Jayden was about to respond when we heard voices coming from the railings on the left side of the rink. I looked over to see Kushaela, Andy, and a few of the other untouchables waving, trying to get Jayden and Kyle's attention.

"Jay-Thor! What's up?" Andy yelled. "What are you guys doing here?"

Jayden skated toward them. "What does it look like? What are ya'll doing here?"

"Just some shopping and then going to a movie." Kushaela looked over toward me and smiled. "Hey Evan, when did you start hanging out with these two troublemakers?"

"He's helping me find Thor, remember?" Jayden had reached the rink's barrier and was looking up at them.

Kyle was close behind him. "And he showed us around the library, his home away from home." Kyle looked back at me, smiling. "He knows every librarian who works there."

Andy couldn't contain his laughter. "How sad." He jumped off the railing and began walking toward the entrance. "I'm going to grab some skates and show you all how it's done."

This was my chance to prove my worth and show them all. I shot out into the crowd where I began skating, gaining momentum as I did a forward crossover and flipped around, gliding backward around the rink.

"Go, Evan!" I heard Kushaela say as I breezed past her.

"He's really good," Jayden commented. "Do that turn again."

You read my mind. I'd just built enough speed to begin my twirl when I thought I saw someone I recognized out of the corner of my eye.

"EVAN JEROD SINCLAIR!" someone yelled from the other side of the rink. I would know that voice anywhere. It was Dad. As I rounded the corner, I spotted him standing at the railing, arms crossed, his nostrils flaring. My stomach rolled, and chills shot through my chest, causing me to lose my footing. I'd been skating so fast that I couldn't halt my momentum, so I was thrust backward and skidded on my back to the other side of the rink while staring up at the roof of the center.

CHAPTER 19

THE EXTRA INNING

Once I came to a halt after my graceful plunge, I tried to quickly jump to my feet, only to slip and find myself on my back again, but this time with an even louder thud. I could hear the snickers of on-lookers around me, but none louder than Andy.

Tears of humiliation began to well up in my eyes, but I refused to cry, not in front of them. I wouldn't give them the satisfaction. I sat up and took a few quick breaths, trying to decelerate my racing heart. I saw a figure standing over me.

"Evan, you OK?" Jayden asked. "Man, that was savage."

Kyle was soon by his side. "Yeah, much more skillful than your first twirl," he quipped.

They both laughed, each one grabbing one of my arms and lifting me onto my feet. I was trying to regain my footing when I heard another voice. "Evan Jerod Sinclair. Get over here now."

Crud! With my stumble, I'd momentarily forgotten all about Dad. And he had used my full given name. This was not going to end well. He was leaning over the railing, and I could hear his heavy breathing all the way down on the rink. I looked at Kyle and Jayden. They looked between Dad and me, and I could see the pity in their eyes. They also knew I was in some serious hot water.

"Gee, your dad sounds peeved," Jayden said, rubbing his eyebrow.

"You don't know the half of it," I said, moving toward the exit.

"Sucks to be you, man." Kyle patted me on the shoulder as I stepped off the rink. "Dude, it's been real. I have a new respect for the library, especially topside." Kyle winked.

Jayden looked from me to Kyle with his brows furrowed. "Yeah," Jayden said. "This place is sick. I'd be up for doing this again."

"Awesome," I said. "I told you guys there was more to the library than most people think." Normally, my heart would have soared because that was exactly what I was hoping they would say. That's why I'd worked so hard to make this perfect. But that supersized tumble and knowing what was in store for me with Dad put a damper on my exuberance.

"Hey, don't forget to let me know if you find out anything else about my bat," Jayden said before turning and skating toward his friends on the other side of the rink.

"I will," I said, defeated. "See you guys Monday." I slowly made my way to the seats to unlace my skates. I couldn't put off the inevitable. I would have to face Dad soon enough. Making him wait even longer would only make things worse, so I hurried my pace.

After returning the skates and putting on my sneakers, I knew it was time to face the consequences, so I exited the ice-skating office, only to run into Andy and Kushaela, and the rest of the gang as they were entering. "Oh my God, Evan, are you ok?" Kushaela said. At least I heard genuine concern in her voice. "That was harsh."

"Man, I haven't laughed that hard in a long time." Andy followed behind her as they all filed to the front counter to, I assumed, join Kyle and Jayden on the rink.

"Give it a rest, Andy." Kushaela scoffed. "Let's see how well you do when we get out there."

I gritted my teeth. This was all dad's fault. He had ruined my concentration, and yet again, I was the laughingstock. Warm ripples rushed throughout my body. Why hadn't he just let Big Momma pick me up later? Who was I kidding? I should have known sending him that text would've only given him more resolve to pick me up.

I didn't even look up to respond to the untouchables. As Big Momma would say, I had bigger fish to fry, and I saw my big fish standing right across from the office with his arms crossed.

"Let's go," Dad said gruffly as he led me to the escalator going down to the parking garage. We stepped onto the escalator, and he turned to look at me. "You OK? That looked like a nasty fall."

"I'm good," I said, almost too quickly. Now, all of a sudden, he was concerned for my well-being. He remained silent until we got in the car. The anticipation was eating me alive, but I was sure that was what he wanted.

"So you do understand English, right?" Dad said, settling into the front seat of the car. "Both American and that King's English you speak all the time?"

"Uh-huh," I said, opening the back door. I thought it would be safer to sit in the back seat, and because I was still feeling completely humiliated, I preferred to have some space to continue wallowing in my embarrassment. *Talk about an epic fail.* I'd done some embarrassing things in my life, but this had to be the most mortifying.

"Excuse me." He turned around, shooting daggers from his eyes.

"Yes, sir," I corrected myself as I climbed into the back seat.

"I just want to be sure because, correct me if I am wrong, but I could have sworn I told you that I didn't want you spending the entire day and night at the library, did I not?"

"Yes, sir, you did."

"So, you deliberately disobeyed me." It sounded more like a statement than a question.

"Dad, I studied all last night for the competition." I curled my lower lip. All this because of a stupid BTU competition. Church always seemed to screw up my life. "Jayden and Kyle wanted to go ice-skating . . ."

"I don't give a crap about Jayden and Kyle. I don't even care if Jesus Christ was on the rink. When I tell you to do something, you do it."

I collapsed into the seat. I knew I wasn't going to win this argument.

"Jayden? Is that the kid who wanted you to help him with that thunder bat thing?"

"Yes, that's him. And it's his lightning bat."

"I don't care if it's his hurricane bat." His voice was now at full volume. "I heard him ask you about it. Well, you best tell him that you're going to be far too busy next week prepping for the upcoming BTU competitions, so you will no longer be able to assist him."

"Dad, I will still have time . . ." I started to protest.

"I don't see how since you will be coming straight home from school every day next week to study your Bible verses, and that includes not going to Big Momma's."

"Dad, you can't . . ."

He abruptly turned to look at me. "I can't do what?" His eyebrows cocked.

I opened my mouth to respond but then thought better of it. I folded my arms against my chest, feeling my heart racing like it was about to leap out of my chest.

"Consequences, my son, consequences. I told you before you don't need to waste your time helping someone find a ridiculous bat. You could be doing something much more productive with your time, like studying for BTU." He chuckled. "I still don't understand why he would ask you."

Anger shot through my body like a cartoon character with smoke coming out of its ears. "Because I'm good at finding stuff and figuring stuff out."

"You are? Since when?"

"Since forever. Mom knew that. You'd know it too if you weren't working all the time." I knew I was throwing daggers, but I didn't care. I wanted to hurt him like he had just hurt me.

"And do you know why I'm working all the time?" he asked, his arms sweeping up and down before the car swerved and he placed them back on the wheel. I stared straight ahead and put my head in my hand. There was no reasoning with him when he got like this.

"I do it so you have a roof over your head, and you can go ice-skating and do all the things you want to do." His eyes tightened. "But you have to meet me halfway. And as long as you live under my roof, you have to respect me and follow my rules."

I slouched down in the seat.

"Are we clear?"

"Yes, sir." His way or the highway, that's the way things always had to be. *I can't wait until I go off to college. He doesn't understand me at all.*

We sat in silence the rest of the way home.

CHAPTER 20

THE CURVEBALL

Sunday morning . . . Ugh . . . I stood in front of the bathroom mirror, fashioning my tie in a full Windsor knot. My eyelids doubled in weight. I'd stayed up most of the night ruminating over yesterday's library kerfuffle. I still couldn't believe I had fallen in front of all the untouchables. This was an all-new low. Since I couldn't sleep and I didn't want to think about the skating rink theatrics, I had stayed up reading the book Kyle had recommended. It was quite the departure from my usual sci-fi adventures. It was the story of Tommy Zane and Mario Santelli, trapeze artists in the '40s and '50s who worked and traveled with a circus. Right from the start, it was full of drama. Tommy was going against his family by being a trapeze artist instead of a lion tamer, and Mario was marrying a woman he didn't love due to family pressure, so they had become allies as Mario showed Tommy the ropes, literally, of becoming a trapeze artist. Surprisingly, the story piqued my interest, but I still didn't understand why Kyle had thought I would enjoy the book so much. However, I was interested enough to keep reading, which was why I could barely keep my eyes open this morning.

I was dressed in a golden-brown suit, which included a jacket and a vest. I hated having to wear a suit, especially a vest and a tie. It made me feel claustrophobic like my circulation was being cut off. I did like the color of my tie. It was light brown, the color of peanut butter, with red accents. It brightened up the suit but consequently choked me at the same time.

"Evan, hurry up. We're gonna be late." Dad walked into the bathroom and adjusted my mangled tie, pulling it tight.

"Ouch." I took a step back.

Dad held tight. I could tell he was still upset about last night. "Man up." He gave the tie one more adjustment and started toward the door. He suddenly stopped short, and I noticed him looking at the framed picture of mom and me on the dresser. It had been taken at the last Rangers games we had attended together before she got really sick. He blinked a few times before he reached over and patted my head. "You have her eyes, you know." He sighed and then clutched my shoulder. "C'mon, let's go, buddy."

Dad and I hurried into the church, late as usual. We even missed Sunday school, which rarely happened. Dad must have had a late night, too, no doubt working on one of his über-important spreadsheets.

I headed to my usual spot, dead center in the middle set of pews. Dad required that I sit right smack in the middle of the sanctuary where I was in full view so he could see me at all times. Dad continued to the front of the church to sit with the other deacons, smiling and patting me on my back as we parted ways like we were best buds or something. That was Dad, always putting on a show. No matter how bad things might be between us, which was contentious at best after last night, we could never air our dirty laundry in public. How uncouth and un-Southern, much like unsweetened tea. Instead, you just grinned and pretended everything was perfect. After years of training, I knew how to play my part all too well. If anything, I was an expert because it was just another mask I was forced to wear to fit in and not appear different.

My nostrils filled with the familiar scent of furniture polish mixed with a potpourri of what I called old-lady fragrances as I sank into the pew. The scent reminded me of all the reasons I dreaded church. The suit and tie were just the start. The uncomfortable wooden bench pews were my second tribulation of the day. You would think after attending as many church services as I had, my bum would be immune to the pain, but it never failed; after only ten minutes in those pews, I would have aches in new, unexplored regions of my backside. This would cause me to squirm in my seat continuously, and after two or three rearrangements, Mom would have given me one of her you-better-be-still-or-else looks. Now I would give anything to see one of those looks again.

After all the choir selections, Pastor Franklin rose and stood be-hind the pulpit, which meant the sermon was starting. Because Dad sat on the front pew with the deacons, he couldn't keep a close watch on me during the service, so he always quizzed me on the main points of the sermon after church, just to make sure I'd been paying atten-tion. This made me even more of a social pariah, especially when all the other kids my age didn't have to sit with their parents and could come and go as they pleased throughout the service.

"So, I ask the question again, are you living your life *right?*" Pastor Franklin questioned the churchgoers with his signature fervent bra-vado. "I see some blank faces out there. Well, don't worry if you aren't quite sure because that is what we are going to discuss this morning."

My ears perked up. That was the information I needed to know to pass the quiz. Now, I just needed the Bible verses the sermon was based on. Dad always asked for that.

"So, if you don't know if you're living life right, let's turn to the one place that tells us everything we need to know and what thus said the Lord. Turn to Timothy Chapter 1 verses 8 through 11."

Perfect! I recorded the information on my phone, so I could refer to it later. Now I could just sit back and relax, tuning everything out until the pastor signaled the conclusion and summed up the entire sermon. That usually gave me more than enough info to pass the test.

This particular Sunday, my enemy was sleep. My eyes would not stay open. I was starting to nod off when I heard the pastor say, "And that includes homosexuals." The woman behind me screamed, "Amen! Hallelujah!" which jolted me wide awake. Oh great, what was the pastor saying about homosexuals this time?

"Do I need to say that again? I think somebody didn't hear me," the pastor reiterated.

I flopped down in my seat, looking around to see if anyone was looking at me.

"Let me read those verses again. The law is not made for a right-eous person, but for the lawless and insubordinate, for the ungodly and sinners, for the unholy and profane, for murderers of fathers and murderers of mothers, for manslayers, for fornicators, for homosexuals, for kidnappers, for liars, for perjurers, and if there is any other thing that is contrary to sound doctrine."

"All right, Reverend. Speak!" The woman behind me was on a roll now.

"So, if you fall into any of the categories I just mentioned, then you are *not* living your life right."

"I hear you, Pastor! Preach!" The woman's voice joined the chorus of acclamations reverberating all over the church.

My leg started trembling. I immediately put my hand on my knee to shut it down before anyone noticed. I knew it was crazy, but I could have sworn that Pastor Franklin was looking right at me. My face tingled as I tried to act natural.

"The verse says the law is not made for the righteous, but for the ungodly and the sinners, meaning those who aren't living their life right, therefore they're not righteous." I could see the pastor was starting to "feel" the holy ghost, as he was smiling from ear to ear and started jumping up and down. "Don't let them fool you with all these gay rights. God made Adam and Eve, not Adam and Steve. You can love homosexuals all you want. God is love, but what they are doing is a sin. They're not the righteous; they're breaking the laws of nature."

Moisture filled my eyes, and I had a thickness in my throat. Being gay meant that you weren't going to Heaven. Being gay meant that people might love you, but they would hate that you loved someone of the same sex. Being gay meant that your family and friends shunned you. *Why would anyone want to be gay? That couldn't be me.* But what about my feelings for Kyle? I couldn't deny those, no matter how hard I tried. I took a few deep breaths and slid further down on the pew. I willed myself not to cry.

My phone vibrated. Thank goodness. I needed something to take my mind off the sermon. It was Angelica. She was not happy with me. *WYD? You didn't call me back last night.* ☹

Sorry. I was knackered. That wasn't exactly the truth. I didn't text her because I didn't want to rehash my embarrassing ice-skating snafu. *At church now, listening to how to live my life right.* I recalled our earlier conversation and thought better of telling her about the true message of the sermon.

I hope ur taking notes! LMAO. 😊 *Call me as soon as u get out.*

I smiled, her message making me less anxious. I responded, *K.* I knew she was dying to know what had happened with Kyle, but texting with her also made me recall her story about her mom fleeing from a church in which the minister gave a similar sermon. I then flashed back to the last words my mom spoke to me, ". . . everything about you is perfect."

A warm sensation flowed down my spine. *I'm not going to sit here and listen to this!* Without giving a second thought to the consequences, I jumped out of my seat and busted out the side door. But as luck would have it, I ran right into my "favorite" churchgoer, Sam Asher, who was hanging with his crew just to the left of the door.

"Look who decided to join us today?" He smirked, pointing at me. "Were you able to sneak away from Daddy?"

"I can do what I want." I stood tall, puffing out my chest because today, of all days, that was true.

"I can do what I want," one of them mocked my inflection.

"He talks so proper. He doesn't know he's black," Sam dug in.

I was accustomed to such comments from the other African-American kids, especially those who went to the church. I couldn't help that I lived in the suburbs, and many of my friends were white. But they never let me live it down.

"What is that supposed to mean?" I knew the answer before he spoke.

"You tell me, Mr. Boot Scootin'."

My cheeks burned. I refused to be chastised over my musical tastes. If anything, I relished my love of country music because it subverted conventional expectations. "It's not my fault you're small-minded."

"Well, then whose fault is it that you're gay?"

My face stung like I had been backhanded. I didn't have many friends at church. Although I'd grown up with many of the teens, they didn't have much to say to me. And those that did ridiculed me, much like Sam. They said I talked funny and was too bougie and acted too effeminate. It was funny how so many people were so quick to tell you who and what you were when you hadn't even figured it out yourself.

I didn't want to engage further. I scurried toward the front of the church, hearing their deafening cackles in my wake when I was startled by a buzz in my pocket. I pulled out my phone and avoided the mad dash of parishioners exiting the church by beelining it to the far-right corner of the building, where there were fewer people.

I looked down at my phone to see that I had a text from a blocked number.

I know who took the bat. Meet me at Sandy Village Park by the big toy at 2:00 p.m. today.

I scratched my forehead. Why all the subterfuge? If someone had a tip, why not just tell me? Unless it was the thief. I desperately needed something to make up for yesterday and get back in Jayden and Kyle's good graces, so nervous or not, I knew without a doubt I was going to the park at 2:00 p.m.

Now the bigger question was, how would I get to the park and then get back in time for the BTU competition?

My phone vibrated again. It was Angelica again. *U out of church yet? I'm dying here.*

My back stiffened. Thank you, Angelica. I knew what I needed to do. I texted Big Momma first.

I'm at church. Can you come get me and take me to Angelica's?

I hoped she had her cell phone nearby. Like Dad, she refused to give up her landline, so she often didn't even take her cell phone out of her purse when she was home.

Dad was counting the offering with the other deacons in the finance room, so I shot him a text next.

Can I go have lunch with Angelica and her parents?

I strategically used Angelica because I knew Dad would approve of my hanging out with her. He knew her parents, and he mistakenly thought I had a crush on her, but more importantly, she also lived near the park, so I could easily meet the mystery caller and maintain my alibi.

While waiting for replies from Dad and Big Momma, I texted Angelica and told her I was going to stop over just in case Dad happened to call. She responded immediately, happy to oblige because she still wanted to hear all the gossip.

My phone vibrated again.

OK. On my way. Be there in 10 min.

Perfect! Big Momma was coming to pick me up. I was about to put the phone back in my pocket when it vibrated again. Dad responded.

OK. Just make sure you're back by 3 for the competition.

Smashing! It had all worked out much easier than I had anticipated. He must have been so focused on the church finances that he just agreed. That was one of the upsides of his being a workaholic. Let's just hope I can make it back by 3:00 for the competition, or I'm snookered.

CHAPTER 21

THE DEAD BALL

"Where's your dad?" Big Momma asked as I slid into the car and buckled my seat belt.

"In the finance room." Being a deacon, Dad was part of the finance team that counted the offerings after church and balanced the books. "He will be in there until BTU starts."

I sat back in the seat, my mind recalling what the pastor had said about living your life right, along with cut-ins of Sam calling me gay. It was the last thing on which I wanted to dwell. I tried to force myself to focus on the case, but no matter how hard I tried, I kept hearing the pastor's and Sam's words in my head, "*It's Adam and Eve, not Adam and Steve*" and "*Can you help it that you're gay?*"

"Why are you looking so glum?" Big Momma asked, glancing between me and the road.

I realized I hadn't said much since she had picked me up. I should have known she would notice. "Nothing, I'm just tired." I didn't want to think about it, much less talk about it.

"Mm-hmm, I'm not buying it. Out with it," she insisted.

"It was just something Pastor Franklin said at church today." Maybe she would leave it at that.

After a few seconds, she stopped at a traffic light and turned to me. "Well, are you going to tell me what he said?"

I looked straight ahead at the dashboard, avoiding her stare. "That if you aren't living your life right, you aren't loved by God."

"Well, that's poppycock! Those Southern Baptists, all about fire and brimstone. My church isn't always much better, but they don't have quite as many absolutes like women shouldn't wear pants or cut their hair. That's just ridiculous."

I had never understood those rules either. Why would God care what you wore and how you styled your hair if you were a good person? But that was something Pastor Franklin mentioned from time to time, even though the majority of women in the congregation wore pants — outside of church, anyway — and cut their hair. "But what if you don't deserve God's love because of who you are, not because of how you look?" My heart began to beat faster.

"Everyone deserves God's love, no matter who they are or what they've done." Big Momma glanced in my direction as she turned on the road. "One thing I have learned about religion is that you take what works for you, and you throw out the rest."

"Really? Can you do that?" Pastor Franklin had never mentioned that. He always made it seem like it was all or nothing.

"Oh, Evan, honey, never forget you're the master of your own life, and it's too short for you not to do the things that bring you happiness, regardless of what anyone says, and that includes me, your dad, and especially some jackass minister."

If anyone was living proof of doing what made her happy, no matter the consequences, it was Big Momma. I took a big sigh of relief as my pulse returned to normal. As usual, Big Momma always knew the right thing to say to make me feel better.

"How are things going with the case?"

"I think I have a new lead." That was all I was willing to say. I knew if I told her about the text, she wouldn't want me to meet this anonymous person in the park. Big Momma supported my sleuthing, but I knew there was a limit.

As Big Momma pulled into the park, I looked down at my watch. One minute till 2:00.

"So, what's this lead?"

"I promise I'll tell you everything, but I'm running late. Angelica is probably looking for me."

"You sure you don't want me to just drop you off at her house?" She only sat up to about the same height as the top of the steering wheel, wearing her bright pink and turquoise caftan.

"I'll be fine. Thanks for the ride."

I jumped out of the car before she could ask any more questions and ran into the park. Nothing seemed out of the ordinary as I quickly scanned the perimeter. A few kids were on the playground, including two young girls around five or six on the swings and two older boys slightly younger than me swinging wildly on the monkey bars.

I sauntered over to the huge, wooden jungle gym, which everyone called the "Big Toy." It stood just less than ten feet tall and included monkey bars, swings, ladders, a rope tunnel bridge, a climbing net, and a covered slide. Trying not to draw attention, I reached the big toy and placed my foot on the climbing net, pretending to brush the dirt off my shoes as I looked around for the anonymous informant.

A mother with a toddler in her arms crossed the playground and headed for the swings. She placed him on one and pointed to the young girls swinging into the high heavens beside him, trying to show him how much fun it was, but it was clear from his crying protests that he wanted no part of it. I was so engrossed in the boy's plight that I barely realized how much time had passed. It was five minutes past two when I looked at my phone.

I didn't see anyone else around, so I decided to walk around to the other side of the big toy, toward the slide's ladder, when I saw a piece of paper taped to the edge of the top rung. I rushed over to it and saw my name scribbled on it. I grabbed the note and looked around the park, but other than parents and the same kids I'd seen earlier, there was no one else around.

How could someone leave this note without me seeing it? I opened it up.

Stop looking for "Thor," or you will be sorry! It's just a bat. Tell Jayden to find another lucky bat. That's what's best for both of you! Consider this your first and last warning!

My breath became heavier as I pressed my fingertips to my forehead. This was the last thing I had expected. I needed a clue, and this was the furthest thing from a lead. Instead, my life was being threatened unless I dropped the case. Oddly enough, that didn't bother me nearly as much as having to tell Jayden that I was right back at square one. This was certainly not going to help me redeem myself after yesterday.

I discarded the note and frantically began running around the big toy to see if I could catch a glimpse of who might have left it. If I didn't come up with something, my chances of being Jayden and Kyle's new bestie were slim to none.

I rabidly circled the big toy several times but failed to spot anyone suspicious. I finally decided to give up and run to Angelica's when I noticed two figures at the north end of the parking lot having what looked like a very animated discussion. It was an older man with a boy who looked to be my age wearing a baseball cap, but I could only see him from behind. The kid was standing in front of the man, so I couldn't make out either one of them. At first, I thought it was a father and son, so I didn't want to stare and make the chap even more self-conscious. I knew how embarrassed I got when I argued with Dad in public. I was about to look away when the boy turned, and I recognized him right away, along with the man he was talking to. Kyle and Coach Bennett.

Why would Kyle and Coach Bennett meet in the park on a Sunday afternoon, especially just the two of them? I knew that Kyle lived close by, so maybe he had come to the park to practice and just ran into the coach. That was a big coincidence. Gibbs on *NCIS* always said there was no such thing as a coincidence. That was another show Mom and I had loved to watch together.

That made me ponder why Kyle would be here alone and not practicing with the other team members. Maybe the coach was giving him private training sessions? But then why did it look like they were arguing?

I had more questions than answers. My brain rattled, trying to make sense of the situation. I debated nonchalantly going up to them to find out what was happening, but given their irate interaction, I thought it best to leave them be. But what if Kyle needed help? Patrick and Jayden had both said they thought the coach was, in Angelica's words, kinda sketchy.

Before I had time to answer that question, Kyle glanced across the parking lot and spotted me. He waved and started running toward me.

There was no escaping it now. Surprisingly, Coach Bennett didn't acknowledge me at all. He glanced over his shoulder, seeing me, then scowled as he scuttled to his car. Maybe he was miffed because the article I was supposedly writing about him hadn't come out yet.

"Hey, E, what are you doing here?" Kyle asked, catching his breath.

"Kyle, what's up, buddy?" I cringed. I was trying too hard again. "I decided to take a walk after church and just ended up here." I didn't want to tell him about the phone call and the note, especially since nothing had come of it.

"Oh, cool. It's a nice day to be out."

"What about you?" I was dying to know. "Everything okay with you and Coach Bennett? Things looked heated." I was trying not to sound too inquisitive.

"Yeah, yeah," he said, almost too quickly. "He's always riding me about being more committed to the team. I was here for my brother's Little League game. He coaches them too."

Okay, now that made sense. "Yeah, I did hear he coached a Little League team."

"He does a good job with them." Kyle looked back over his shoulder as if he needed to confirm the coach had departed. "My mom took them all out for ice cream, so she should be back to pick me up any minute."

Kyle's eyes finally met mine. "I just didn't want to be around a bunch of screaming seven- and eight-year-olds."

"I hear ya." We both laughed. "I better get going anyway. I'm sure my dad is wondering where I am." I had to haul it over to Angelica's so her parents could get me back to church in time for BTU.

"Speaking of your dad, did you recover from that tumble yesterday?" he laughed.

My cheeks burned. "Don't remind me."

His voice softened, "Hey, have you started the book yet?"

"Yeah, I did. It was a bit slow to start, but I like it so far."

"See, I told you," he said as he reached out and gripped my shoulder. After a few seconds, I noticed that Kyle was holding the grip.

"BTW, we should do the library again sometime." He smiled and still didn't let go. Kyle's hand was warm and strong, and I could feel his batting calluses through my shirt as he gave me a firm squeeze.

I tried not to squirm. I wasn't sure what was happening, but the elation almost caused me to lose my balance.

Kyle winked. "Maybe next time, it can just be the two of us. See you at school tomorrow." He finally released his grasp before running to the other side of the parking lot.

My head spun with confusion when I suddenly noticed a figure lurking in the brush just to the left of the big toy. I couldn't quite tell who it was, but then I caught a glimpse of his face. It was Christian Carlson, Jayden's nemesis on the team. How long had he been there? Had he been the one who left the note? It certainly sounded like something he would write.

I began walking toward the big toy when Christian noticed my approach and trampled into the bushes, running behind the park. What was that all about? Why would he run away from me? Perhaps after our altercation the other day, he thought it best to stay clear of me. Christian and his doctor's appointment alibi were getting shakier and shakier. He was hiding something. *I'll find out what you're hiding, Christian. You can bet on that.*

CHAPTER 22

THE CALLED STRIKE

"It took you long enough," Angelica said as she opened the front door. "You look a hot mess."

"You can say that again." I was cramped over from the stitch in my side. I hadn't realized that I'd been at the park for over twenty minutes until I had looked at my phone. I hightailed it over to Angelica's in record time with my phone clutched in my hand. I'd taken it out of my pocket to keep it from weighing me down.

I panted my way into a large foyer filled with exotic Japanese art. Angelica's father was quite a collector. "Are your parents here? I need them to get me to church and fast. It's already after 2:30," I spat out between short, quick breaths. "If I miss the competition, my dad'll kill me."

"Yeah, Dad's in the garage babying his new car. He's been looking for any excuse to get behind the wheel." Angelica beckoned for me to follow her into the living room. Her house was always meticulously clean, with everything in its place. Considering that the carpeting, sofa, and chaise longue were all solid white, that was no small feat.

My hand was cramping from clenching the phone so tightly. I plonked it onto the kitchen counter and made a mental note to remember to retrieve it before we left.

"I'll get you some tea, and you start spilling yours." She took a pitcher out of the refrigerator before opening a cabinet, grabbing an electric blue glass goblet and filling it to the rim.

"He was weird. He kept bringing up gay people." I looked around to make sure her dad wasn't listening as I recounted my interactions with Kyle at the library, including his comments about Zachary Quinto and the two "gay" ice-skaters hanging on to each other.

She placed the goblet in front of me as I sat at the kitchen table. "See, I told you he's next level extra."

"Yeah, then he asked me if I thought there was something wrong with two guys liking each other."

Angelica's eyes bugged out. "Shut the front door! What did you say?"

"Jayden was flirting with this girl at the rink, and he came back before I could say anything."

Angelica rolled her eyes again. "Of course he was. He thinks he's such a player."

I grinned. "He got her phone number." I leaned in closer to Angelica. "So, do you think Kyle might be . . .?" I raised my eyebrows, hoping Angelica knew what I meant.

"Gay?" Angelica said louder than I would have liked, causing me to quickly pan the room.

"I don't know about gay, but I do think he's cray-cray." Angelica knitted her brows. "I think he's saying those things to find out if you're gay so he can go back and tell everyone at school just to humiliate you."

"I don't know."

"Oh wow . . . You've got it bad."

I stared down at my tea. "I have no idea what you're talking about."

"Uh-huh. So let me ask you something. How do you feel about two guys liking each other?"

I shifted my weight from one foot to the other. "What?" I kept my head down to avoid looking at her. "I don't know. I don't think about that kind of stuff."

"Why not?"

My face flushed. "Why should I? It doesn't have anything to do with me."

"Sure, it doesn't, but you do acknowledge that two guys can like each other, and there's nothing wrong with that, no matter what your dad or your cockamamie minister says."

I cleared my throat, finally looking at her. "Yeah, of course." A sudden calmness overtook me.

"So . . . sounds like Kyle is turning on the charm."

I noticed a twinkle in her eyes, suddenly realizing what she was implying. "It's not like that," I said, almost too quickly. My pulse accelerated. "I don't like him that way."

"What-ev-er." She pursed her lips. "You can't trust him, and whatever you do, don't tell him anything, or you'll regret it."

"I have nothing to tell him."

"Uh-huh," Angelica said while rolling her eyes.

"That's only half the story. I just ran into him at Sandy Village. He was there with Coach Bennett. He said they were practicing. But when we were talking, he grabbed my shoulder and held onto it for a long time, saying we should go to the library again, just the two of us."

Angelica firmly placed her glass on the counter. "I can't even . . . He is totally playing you. Promise me you won't get sucked into his mind games." Angelica raised her hand and extended her pinky finger toward me. "Pinky swear?"

I hooked fingers with hers. "Pinky swear."

After that, I filled her in on all the other developments in the case, including how I had seen Christian making his very suspicious getaway from the park.

I wasn't sure how much time had passed as I reached over to grab my phone from the back counter. I gasped. It was already after 3:00 p.m. I'd had no idea we'd been chitchatting that long. I already had three messages from Dad.

Where r u?

U better be on ur way,

Competition is starting. You're in big trouble, mister.

Bloody heck! I'd forgotten to take the phone off silent after church. OMG! As Big Momma had told me the time I ate one of her favorite candy bars without asking, I was in serious hot water, and it was boiling over.

CHAPTER 23

THE SWITCH HITTER

I'd have rather stuck my hand in a barrel of rattlesnakes than enter the church when Mr. Tyler and I finally arrived. Poor guy, he'd almost run two stoplights trying to get me here, but it was already after 3:30 when we finally arrived. Since I'd already given Angelica the 411, she had opted not to ride with us. She'd said she didn't want to see me get murdered. Good call because that could very well happen.

My dad hadn't been happy when I had texted and told him I was on my way. He hadn't even responded, which meant he was saving his true wrath for when he saw me in person. Even Mr. Tyler had tried to text and tell him that it had been his fault because he had been tinkering with his car, but his response hadn't been much better.

No worries, Jim. It's not your fault. I'll take care of Evan when I see him.
When I'd seen that, I'd known I was done for.

I saw most of the congregation exiting as I reached for the door. Since BTU was always the final service on Sunday evenings, it usually only lasted 30–45 minutes. Why did Dad have to be the very first person I saw when I walked into the church? He was bending over between the pews, picking up leftover programs from the events. When he stood up and saw me, I could feel the arrows spewing from his eyes. He reached into his pocket and threw his car keys toward me. I flinched but surprisingly caught them with one hand. "Go wait in the car," he snapped. "I'll be there as soon as we finish cleaning up."

He didn't have to tell me twice. I quickly turned around and barreled through the main entrance. I let out a huge breath; at least I had a bit more time before I got my tongue-lashing. But even still, I wasn't looking forward to yet another contentious car ride.

I got into the back seat. My thoughts drifted as I waited for the inevitable. I had so many questions: Why had Christian been at the park, and why had he run away when he'd seen me? What had caused the kerfuffle between Kyle and Coach Bennett? Why was Kyle suddenly being über nice to me, and should I heed Angelica's warnings? And most importantly, had my acrobatic fail at the ice rink ruined my chances of hanging out with Jayden, Kyle, and the rest of the untouchables?

I got lost in my contemplations and almost choked when I heard a knock at the window. "Unlock the door." I recognized Dad's voice. Oh no, here we go.

I pressed the unlock button, and Dad opened the back door, tossing in his suit jacket and Bible before getting in the front seat. He started the engine and proceeded to exit the parking lot. My legs trembled as I waited for him to say something. We drove for a full ten minutes and still not a word. I'd prepared myself for one of his mundane speeches, so his speechlessness was driving me bonkers.

Finally, when we were getting on the freeway, I had to breach the silence. "Look, Dad, I'm so sorry about missing the competition." I looked down at my hands in my lap.

He said nothing. I finally looked up to see he was concentrating on the road and wasn't paying me any attention. "Dad, I said I'm sorry. Aren't you going to say anything?"

He finally looked at me, and, to my bewilderment, I didn't see anger but sadness in his eyes. "What do you want me to say, Evan?"

"I don't know. Yell at me or something." My voice was getting higher. My lips were shaking.

"I honestly don't know what else to say to you that I haven't already said, other than the fact I am very disappointed in you."

That hurt my heart more than a scolding ever could. I could feel a lump forming in my throat. "I'm sorry. I know how important BTU is to you. Things just happened that were out of my control."

"Don't do that. Don't blame others for your choices. Yes, Mr. Tyler working on his car was beyond your control, but leaving to go have lunch with them was your choice. And don't think I forgot that you didn't even text me when you got there. How many times have I told you about that? So be a man and own up to your mistakes."

"Yes, sir." This was the tone I had been expecting from him. I didn't even want to think about how furious he would be if he knew the truth.

"So, as a consequence, I am taking your phone for a week."

"Dad . . . "

"You just missed a BTU competition. Do you know how embarrassing that was? I led the group, and my own son was not there to participate. How do you think that makes me look?"

I bit my lip. Of course, it always came back to his precious reputation.

"So, no phone for a week. It's not like you're even using it to stay in contact, which was the entire point of you getting it in the first place."

I looked straight ahead, puckering my lips.

"Are we clear?"

I wanted to say "crystal," but I knew how flippant that would sound, so I just said, "Yes, sir," and slouched down in my seat.

Once again, silence all the way home.

I ran to my room as soon as we arrived and fell onto the bed. Since Dad had confiscated my phone and I wasn't quite tired yet, I decided to dive into the book before taking a shower. After my encounter with Kyle in the park, I wanted to impress him with how far I had gotten.

When I got to page 209, I bolted upright in bed, almost dropping the book. I could barely believe what I had just read. Tommy and Mario, the main characters in the book, shared a bed in the circus tent because their trapeze practice ran late as usual, but somehow this time, in the middle of the night, they had ended up passionately kissing one another. Wait. What had just happened? They were two guys . . . And they were kissing? OMG, they were gay. A tingling sensation traveled from the top of my spine down to my groin. My stomach swarmed with confusion. I felt guilty, like I should have stopped reading, but I couldn't. I had to find out what was going to happen next. It turned out that they began having a love affair.

I looked around the room as if I was about to be caught red-handed. I couldn't even imagine what my dad would say if he knew what I was reading, especially after today's church sermon. Pastor Franklin had used the term abomination quite a few times. He had said people engaging in such relationships were not living their life according to God's plan, but the thought of Mario and Tommy together seemed very natural and even right to me. Pastor Franklin could be wrong, right? Angelica and Big Momma certainly thought so.

But more than anything, I wondered why Kyle had recommended this book to me, particularly given all the gay references he had been making. Maybe Kyle was gay? Or was Angelica right, and he was toying with me? Even with the uncertainty, I fell asleep with a smile on my face that night.

CHAPTER 24

THE RELIEVER

Barely conscious, I made my way down the hall to history class. There were two things I'd always disliked: mornings and history. Together they were practically unbearable.

This Monday morning was even worse because I'd stayed up reading over 200 pages of the book. I was fascinated by how the two male protagonists had discovered their feelings for one another and how they wanted to be together but had to keep it a secret because they were afraid of their families' reactions. I particularly related to that fear. I was completely drawn to these characters; it was a connection, unlike anything I'd known before, leaving me with a surreal feeling of euphoria combined with trepidation.

I was jolted from my apprehensive thoughts when I saw Andy standing outside his locker, dressed in his typical school-issued tracksuit. I was reminded of what Kyle had said about his possibly being a suspect. I didn't know Andy very well, but in the few interactions we had, he had never failed to clarify how low I was on the social food chain, sea levels below his jock status. My recent ice-skating mishap being a perfect example. But he was friends with Jayden, and he knew that Jayden had tasked me with getting his bat, so hopefully, this one time, he would at least acknowledge my existence.

"Hey, Andy!" I said, my voice shaky.

He spun around, seeing me, before promptly turning his attention back to his locker. His curly hair was a bit longer than usual, hanging down onto his forehead. "What do you want, Sinclair?"

I let out a huge breath when I realized he left out the "sissy" part. "I wanted to talk to you about Jayden's bat."

"What about it?" he said, still not turning to face me.

"So, what's with this bet you had with Jayden?"

He looked at me and scowled. Now I had his attention. "I know what you're getting at, but I had nothing to do with it. Like I would steal a bat to win a dumb bet. It wasn't that serious."

I wasn't sure I believed him, but I thought it best to change tactics. "Of course not," my voice shot up an octave, "but you were there the day it went missing, so I thought maybe you might have seen something that could help me find out who took it."

His face slightly softened. "I didn't see anything."

I needed more elaboration. I tried to channel my inner Veronica Mars, who would never take no for an answer.

"There was no one else around his locker?" I was grasping at straws, but I needed some kind of lead.

"Nope," he said matter-of-factly.

Could he be stonewalling me because he took the bat? Maybe he was also jealous of Jayden's fame and wanted him out of the spotlight, friend or no friend.

I was about to walk away when I heard him say, "The only thing I remember from that day is Coach Bennett talking to some dude. It looked like they were about to go fist city."

I quickly pivoted back toward him. "Do you know who he was?"

"No clue."

"What did he look like?"

"Not sure. But he was dressed in a suit. I do remember that." He slammed his locker. "See ya, Sinclair. I gotta get to class." He bolted down the hall.

He still didn't put the sissy in front of my name. I smiled and walked to class.

When class ended, I jetted to my locker, where I found Jayden waiting for me. "Evan, there you are."

Crikey! Jayden clearly wanted an update on the case. After the clandestine park meeting and my interrogation of Andy, I had hoped I would have something more concrete to tell him. Unfortunately, all I could tell him was Christian had possibly threatened me with a note warning me to drop the case — and given Jayden's disdain for Christian, I didn't want to fan those flames without solid proof — or that his BFF Andy could be a suspect, which wouldn't go over well either.

I had to solve this case, or else my plans to join the untouchables would never come to fruition. I was trying to think of what to say when Jayden clutched my shoulder, pulling me around to face him.

"I'm stoked. I heard about the big break in the case. Let me know when you find it. I can't wait to get Thor back and get back on my winning streak. You rock!"

Flustered, I rubbed my ear as my nose crinkled. "Uh . . . um . . . what?"

Jayden tilted his head and laughed. "It's all good. I ran into Patrick this morning, and he told me everything."

Patrick had done what? Now I was even more perplexed. Why would he be talking to Jayden, and especially on my behalf? My jaw clenched. Now Jayden knew Patrick was helping me with the case. That had been the last thing I wanted.

A voice in the now very crowded hallway screamed, "Hey, Jayden, over here."

Jayden turned back to me. "Keep me posted. I'm counting on you." He gave me a strong slap on the back before he darted into the horde.

I stopped in the middle of the swarm of bodies in the hallway, smelling hairspray, gum, and pungent body odor all at the same time, trying to wrap my head around what had just happened. I suddenly realized where I was and pushed my way through the maze of students. I had to get to the bottom of this immediately. I dashed to the cafeteria to find Patrick and root out what he had told Jayden.

I had just grasped the cafeteria door handle when I spied Lammy coming out of the admin office across the hall. I still needed to find out why Lammy hadn't told me about the altercation Kyle'd said he'd had with Jayden. No better time than the present. I released the handle and zigzagged across the hallway. "Hey, Lammy, you got a sec?"

"Not really," he said, trying to sidestep around me.

I veered, blocking his path. "I promise I'll make it fast."

Lammy's nostrils flared as he glared at me. "Is this about that bogus bat again?"

This wasn't a time for pleasantries, so I would have to do this Wallander-style. He was one detective who never had time for pleasantries. "So why didn't you tell me that you and Jayden had words the day before Thor went missing?"

"Because it's none of your business."

"Why were you two squabbling?"

"I don't have to tell you anything."

I clenched my jaw, knowing I was going to have to play hardball. "It'd be terrible if the principal heard you had something to do with Thor's disappearance. I wouldn't want to jeopardize your working with the team." I hit him below the belt, but I knew his position with the team meant everything to him. I had no choice but to use it as leverage.

His mouth flew open. "You wouldn't do that."

"I don't want to. I just need you to tell me what happened."

"Fine. Jayden threw a hissy fit when I accidentally picked up Thor while I was cleaning up the diamond. I didn't realize it was his lucky bat." Lammy used air quotes when he said "lucky." "I immediately gave it back to him, but not before he called me an idiot and told me to stay away from his stuff. I replied with a few choice words, but that was it. We both went our separate ways."

"Why didn't you tell me about this earlier?"

"I knew how it would look." He looked me straight in the eye. "I'm telling you, I didn't take his bat."

I could see the desperation in his eyes. My intuition told me that he was telling the truth.

"Let me guess, Kyle told you about the confrontation."

I nodded. "Why do you ask?"

"Did he also tell you about his blowup with Coach Bennett?"

"Huh?" I grunted; my eyebrows arched.

"Yeah, I figured as much." Lammy stepped closer to me, lowering his voice to a whisper. "I wasn't going to say anything, but since he ratted me out, I don't mind returning the favor. A couple of days after Thor went missing, I heard the coach and Kyle having a screaming match down in the dugout. I couldn't make out the entire conversation, but I heard the coach say, 'We do this my way, or you'll regret it.'"

My lips went cold. Yet another heated conversation between the coach and Kyle, just like the one I'd witnessed in the park. That couldn't be a coincidence. "Do you have any idea what they were talking about?"

"Not a clue. At the time, I thought it had something to do with his position on the team, but now that I think about it, it could have had something to do with Jay's bat."

I grabbed his forearm. "Thanks, Lammy. I appreciate your telling me. And you do know I never would've said anything to Principal Albert."

Lammy flashed a half-smile. "I know. I should've told you everything from the beginning." He turned and started down the hallway. "I gotta get to the gym before class. I do hope you find the bat."

What could Coach Bennett and Kyle have discussed so emphatically, and more importantly, why had it happened twice? I shoved those thoughts into the back of my mind because, right now, I had to focus on getting to the bottom of what Patrick had told Jayden. I whisked across the hall into the cafeteria.

Just as I expected, I found him with his skater friends all holed up in the back of the cafeteria, sitting on the floor next to their boards. Patrick glimpsed me from across the room and waved his hand. I stomped across the room, my jaw set, ready to lay into him for talking to Jayden without me. I opened my mouth when Patrick said, "Hey, *amigo*, I'm guessing from the look on your face you have talked to Jayden."

My brows furrowed. I wanted to wring his neck. "You bet I have. What the bloody hell did you tell him? He thinks I have a big break in the case—"

Patrick interrupted me, "But that's just it; you do. You just don't know it yet." He smiled.

"What?" I twisted and rubbed my hands together. This was going to ruin what little rep I had with the untouchables. "I told you that your help with the case had to remain a secret. Jayden and Kyle have to think I'm solving it alone."

"E, come on." Patrick rolled his head from one side to the other. "Who cares what they think?"

I wanted to say, "I do," but with my current lackluster leads, I needed Patrick, and he obviously knew something. I decided it was in my best interest to play nice. I was tempted to divulge the information I'd gleaned from Andy and Lammy, but given how Patrick already felt about Kyle, I didn't want to open those floodgates just yet.

"I appreciate your help, Pat. I'm just dealing with a lot right now."

"Kk, I get that. That's why I'm here to help. Would I ever lead you astray?" I almost laughed at how he was now using my phrases. "I told you, I'm the Watson to your Holmes."

"Then you better start talking, and fast, Dr. Watson," I said with more humor than I had intended. "Let's go over there." Even though Jayden knew Patrick was helping me with the case, I didn't want the entire school thinking we were hanging out again. We moved to the side of the cafeteria near the rear entrance, where it was less noisy, and no one could see us together.

Patrick began to explain. "So the other night, you told me that when you interviewed Coach Bennett, he said that he also coached a Little League team."

"Yep, that's right."

"Well, guess whose little brother plays on that team?"

"You mean Ethan?" Now I was intrigued.

"Exactamente, my pip-squeak of a brother. I was talking to him about how practice had gone yesterday, and he mentioned how one of his teammates wouldn't stop going on about having a lucky lightning bat."

"A lightning bat . . . Wait, you don't think it's Jayden's?"

"The thought did cross my mind." Patrick couldn't contain his smug grin. "You said that Coach Bennett lied about being in the locker room when the bat went missing, and suddenly a kid he is coaching in Little League 'coincidentally' finds a 'lucky' bat." He used air quotes around coincidentally and lucky.

"Pat, you're a genius."

"I've been telling you that for years." Patrick grinned, putting his hand on my shoulder. "I've missed this. It's like old times. We're crushing this case." He stared straight into my eyes, holding the gaze a little longer than usual. My pulse spurred as I looked away.

Noticing my discomfort, he released my shoulder and changed the subject. "Pick up your phone some time, and I could have told you all this when I called you fifty million times last night."

My face fell. "My dad confiscated my phone."

"Huh? Why?" Patrick curled his lips.

"It's a long story. I'll fill you in later." I didn't want to think about that right now because I wasn't going to let that little detail derail my excitement as I bounced from one foot to the other.

"So we need to get to one of Ethan's practices and find out who this new wonder kid is and hope that he leads us to this lucky bat."

"I think I have that covered," Patrick smirked. "What's Big Momma's number?"

CHAPTER 25

THE SCREWBALL

I sat in class waiting for the final bell to ring, unable to stop my foot from tapping uncontrollably. Was I finally going to solve the case? I could hardly wait to see what Jayden would do when I showed up with the bat.

I pictured myself sitting with Jayden and his friends in the cafeteria, hanging out with them after school at the mall, and, of course, watching movies with them at the library every Saturday. Jayden, Kyle, and I would be walking tall down the hall, laughing and slapping each other on the back.

Suddenly, the bell rang, whipping me back into reality. I sprang upright and started shoving my papers and books into my backpack—time to put this case to bed.

I bolted from the classroom. I had a loose end I needed to tie up before meeting Patrick. I trotted down the back hallway to the shop area. As soon as I stepped into the classroom, I was met with the sounds of machines buzzing and the smell of sawdust.

I immediately spotted Christian bent over something like a penthouse for upper-class sparrows.

"Hey, I need to talk to you."

Christian, cleaning up the wood shavings at his workstation, looked over his shoulder to see me coming his way. He grimaced like he wanted to make another run for it, just like he had done in the park yesterday.

"What the hell are you doing here, Sissy Sinclair? You looking for another trip to the nurse's office?" Christian scowled. "You know, you never got back to me about those quotes for that story."

Dang, I had forgotten all about that fake newspaper story. "Yeah, sorry about that. I've been kinda busy. I'm still trying to figure out who took Jayden's bat." I didn't have time to waste. "I would've gotten the quotes from you yesterday when I saw you at the park, but I guess you were in a hurry."

Christian turned back toward his workstation. "I don't know what you're talking about. I'm busy here. Don't you have to go kiss Jayden's butt?"

"Well, you can save us both a lot of time if you just give Jayden his bat back. I know it was you who left me the note." I wasn't sure where my confidence was coming from, but I needed to know why Christian had been at the park, and this was the fastest way to do it. It always worked in crime shows, especially when Sherlock did it, so I elected to channel him.

Before the words were completely out of my mouth, Christian had grabbed the collar of my shirt and yanked me close until our faces were only inches apart. "Bullcrap. I did no such thing, and you better not be spreading lies about me." I smelled peanut butter on his breath and saw beads of sweat forming on his forehead.

At that moment, I was seriously rethinking that technique. It might have been the quickest tactic, but apparently, not the safest. I didn't want a repeat of what had happened last time, but I'd gone too far now to turn back. "Then why were you at the park?"

Christian's face didn't soften. His grip grew tighter.

"Fine, I can always get Principal Albert involved. He takes threats of any kind very seriously. And considering this is your second altercation with me, plus your pugnacious history, I am willing to bet he won't treat you kindly." I smirked, remembering how Big Momma always told me how unkindly she would treat me when I got cheeky with her.

Christian loosened his grip and stepped back. "Pug-what? Speak English, dorkwad."

"Your tendency to start fights."

He still looked confused, but his face finally relaxed. "I told you. I didn't threaten you."

"Then why did you run away?"

"I knew how it would look. Everyone is saying I took it." Christian raised his volume as he balled his fists. "Jayden's a conceited jerk, but I'd rather he gets all the attention than that douche Andy."

I wasn't quite sure what to make of that, but for the moment, I decided to give Christian the benefit of the doubt. "Okay, so if you didn't take the bat or leave me the note, why were you at the park?"

"I was there because I overheard that faker Kyle talking to the coach after practice Friday. They said something about a bat and that they were meeting at the park on Sunday." His eyes shot me daggers. "I was there trying to clear my name, and I would have if you hadn't shown up and spooked them after you made goo-goo eyes at Kyle." Christian scrunched up his nose, not at all hiding his disgust.

Dangit! Did everyone at school think I was crushing on Kyle? My face grew hot, my heartbeat soaring as I stared down at the piles of sawdust covering the floor. "It's not like that . . ." I stopped, suddenly realizing I didn't need to explain myself to Christian. He wouldn't believe me anyway and would likely just mock me more.

"Once Kyle dogged it over to you, Russell's dad came up, and the coach handed him something before they all took off." He turned back to his workstation.

"Wait? Who came up to him?" I asked, my curiosity piqued. How had I missed that? I must have been preoccupied talking with Kyle.

"Russell's dad, I don't know his name. I just see him with Russell at the games."

"Russell?" Why did that name sound familiar? I bit my lower lip as a memory flickered in my head. Kyle had mentioned some guy named Russell was Jayden's nemesis. "Does Russell go here?"

Christian shook his head. "No, he goes to Western."

Yep, that was him, alright. "What's Russell's last name?"

Christian furrowed his brow. "Harden, I think. Or something like that."

"Did you see what Russell's dad gave him?"

"No idea. An envelope or something."

Another revelation clanged in my head. "Was he wearing a suit?"

Christian turned to face me. "Yes, why? What's with the twenty questions? All I know is *I* had nothing to do with that missing bat."

I presumed that was probably all the information I would get out of Christian, but my mind was racing again. Why would the coach be talking to the parent of a kid from Western? And Jayden's nemesis no less? Maybe he had been trying to recruit Russell to Lincoln. Or maybe they had been discussing the championship game. But why would he be talking to a parent about that and not Western's baseball coach? And what had been in the envelope? And the biggest clue yet was the suit. Every guy the coach had run-ins with was wearing a suit. Could it be the same guy?

With the new information Christian provided still germinating in my head, I jetted out of the classroom without uttering another word. I was running late to meet Patrick and Big Momma. We had a Little League practice to crash.

CHAPTER 26

THE KNUCKLER

"*What?*" Patrick's voice was at a fever pitch. "You got an anonymous phone call telling you to go to the park, and you found a threatening letter that you thought Christian wrote, and then you go question him alone after what happened last time?"

Patrick had been talking a mile a minute since I'd met him on the sidewalk outside the school and proceeded to catch him up on the case, including my recent brush with Christian.

"E, are you crazy? You did all that alone? Why didn't you call me? You shouldn't be taking chances like that by yourself."

"There wasn't time. And I told you my dad took my phone." That was relatively true, but he was right. I'd been keeping him at arm's length.

Honestly, I was a bit taken aback. I could see the distress in Patrick's wide eyes. I'd thought for sure Patrick would be more disturbed by the fact I was working the case without him than concerned for my safety.

"Look, I know we're doing this on the DL, but you told me we were working this case together. That means we take the risks together. No more going off on your own." Patrick stepped in front of me, using his skateboard to block my path. "Comprende?"

"Comprende." I was taken aback by Patrick's outburst. That was the most worked-up I'd seen Patrick since I'd eaten the last pudding cup when we had been in second grade.

Big Momma's SUV pulled up to the curb. I wasted no time jumping into the passenger's seat while waiting for Patrick to put his board in the back and climb in the backseat so we could get going.

"So what time does this practice start?" Big Momma asked as Patrick closed the back door, and she began driving slowly down the residential road. She always took the backstreets, avoiding the major roads and freeways at all costs. She said people drove too crazily, and it was better to arrive late and safe rather than not at all.

"Usually 3:45, right after the kids get out of school," Patrick piped from the back seat.

"Evan, you should have texted me earlier. You know how long it takes me to get ready. Patrick just called me half an hour ago."

From the passenger's seat, I could see Big Momma leaning forward as she moderately accelerated the car. "Dad took my cell phone."

"What? Why?" She glared at me. "What did you do?"

"It's a long story." I didn't want to talk about it.

"He missed the church competition yesterday," Patrick volunteered.

I turned, my eyes narrowed, shooting flares at Patrick. "OK, maybe it's not such a long story."

"Oh, dear Lord, it is a wonder you're still alive. You know how your father is about that church." Her eyes brightened. "Wait a second, this doesn't have anything to do with my taking you to Angelica's, does it?"

"Sorta," I said, knowing full well that would not be enough of an explanation.

"You better start talking, Evan, or I will stop this car right here, right now," Big Momma said, slightly raising her voice.

"I did go to Angelica's, but first I was supposed to meet someone at the park who said they knew who stole Jayden's bat."

"But whoever it was didn't show up," Patrick's mouth kept flapping. I turned and shot him another look. At least he hadn't said anything about the threatening note. Big Momma would've freaked out.

"Wait . . . So let me get this straight — you ended up missing church, getting in trouble, and getting your phone taken, all for nothing."

"Basically," I said, slumping down in my seat.

"Well, not exactly; you did run into Kyle and Coach Bennett. And Christian was there creeping." Patrick seemed intent on spilling all the beans.

"And there's that." This time I didn't even bother turning around. I leaned in closer to Big Momma. "Also, can we keep this between us? Technically, I'm grounded, and I'm supposed to go straight home after school."

"What?!" Big Momma stopped the car in the middle of the street. "You're just now telling me this. You know how your father is, and now I'm an unwitting accomplice." Her eyes burrowed into me. "He told you to stop sleuthing, didn't he?"

Darn it; she knew Dad too well. "Yeah, he did, but I am so close, Big Momma. This practice holds the final piece for me to complete the puzzle. I just know it." I folded my arms against my chest. "Besides, I promised Jayden I would get it back. And a promise is a promise. You taught me that."

Big Momma took a deep breath, finally steering the car forward. "For the life of me, I will never understand why this is so important to you."

"I don't get it either," Patrick interjected. I turned around and ran my finger across my neck, signaling him to pipe down. Why was he so talkative all of a sudden? But Big Momma had always said that he couldn't hold water. It was one of his most refreshing characteristics, but at the moment, it was quite annoying.

Big Momma looked up at the rearview mirror and smiled at Patrick. She then parked the car beside the elementary school, pulled the lever into park, and turned to look at me. "I just want what is best for you, and if this will make you happy, then I will help you find this bat." She pointed her finger at me. "If you promise me this is your last act of sleuthing for this case, then I will keep this between us." My lips began to part, revealing my teeth, but Big Momma wasn't finished. "I'm serious. I might not agree with your father, but I won't lie to him or for you. You hear me, Mr. Matlock?"

Bollocks! I couldn't lose Big Momma's support. "Thanks, Big Momma. I hear you loud and clear." I reached over and gave her a peck on the cheek. I heard a chuckle from the back seat. I glared at Patrick before turning back to Big Momma. "I'm glad you're on board because I am going to need your help."

As Big Momma, Patrick, and I cut across the playground to get to the baseball field, we could already hear raised voices. It sounded like adults more than little kids. As we rounded the corner to see the field, we saw the parents sitting on the bleachers yelling to their kids, most used words of encouragement, but a few said things like "Pay attention" and "Come on, hustle, hustle." It reminded me of my dad when he regrettably put me in Little League.

"There he is, over there, behind the batting cage," Patrick said, pointing toward the backstop.

I instantly spotted Ethan bouncing around the backstop with the other players, looking like a miniature version of Patrick with the same bright green eyes, but his hair was more light brown compared to Patrick's jet-black curls.

Patrick approached the fence and whistled the *Doctor Who* theme. Recognizing the call, Ethan turned around, grinned from ear to ear, and skipped from around the backstop to join us on the side of the bleachers.

"Hey, Patty, what are you doing here? It's not time to go," he said with a wide gap showing off his missing front tooth.

"Hey, pip-squeak, I told you not to call me that in public."

Ethan's eyes grew bigger. "Oh, sorry. I forgot."

I grinned. "It's okay, Ethan. I call him Patty all the time."

"Do you remember my friend Evan?"

Ethan nodded. "Si, he used to come over, and we'd watch cartoons together."

"That's right." Patrick waved his hand toward Big Momma. "And this is Evan's grandmother, Big Momma."

"Big Momma? That's a funny name." Ethan beamed.

Big Momma smiled. "Is it? So what do you call your grandmother?"

"*Abuelita.*"

"Well, that sounds pretty funny to me too," Big Momma tittered.

Patrick cleared his throat and got us back on track. "So, Ethan, where is that kid you were telling me about with the new lucky bat?"

He squinted his eyes. "Oh, Jimmy. He can't find his bat, so he won't play anymore."

"WHAT?" Patrick and I shouted in unison. My heart splattered on the ground beneath me.

Ethan, startled, dropped his jaw and took a step back. "He lost his bat, so he's mad. He's sitting over there." He pointed over to a kind-of chubby red-haired kid slumped on the front bleacher like he had just lost his will to live.

"Thanks, *hermanito*. You better get back to practice now."

Ethan waved at us and headed back to the batting area. "Bye, Patty! Bye, Evan! Bye, Big Momma!"

I flipped around and doubled over, feeling like the wind had been knocked out of me. "How could he have lost that bat?" I was bewildered.

"E, we'll figure this out."

Big Momma rubbed my back. "Don't get your panties in a bunch. There is always more than one way to skin a cat. Think about what we know. This boy had the bat, so he had to have gotten it from somewhere."

"True. I have to talk to him," I said, standing upright. "But we need to distract Coach Bennett." I eyed Big Momma.

"Oh dear, not again." Big Momma said, looking between Patrick and me.

"Here's what I need you to do," I whispered my plan into Big Momma's ear.

Big Momma walked out to the middle of the field, where Coach Bennett appeared to be giving the eight-year-old shortstop tips on how to catch a grounder. "Hi, Coach Bennett; I'm Ruth Anderson, chair of the neighborhood watch committee. Can I have a moment of your time?"

The coach barely looked at Big Momma before turning back to the player. "For Christ's sake, can this wait? I'm a little busy here," the coach said sullenly.

"No, I'm afraid not," Big Momma spoke sternly to match the coach's temperament. "Some of the parents are very concerned about the children's safety after practice."

"In what way?" The coach turned to Big Momma, finally giving her his full attention.

"They are worried about the children being left unattended after practice." She pointed to the opposite side of the field, away from the bleachers. "Can we talk about this over here?"

"What? That never happens on my watch," the coach said, crossing his arms as he walked over to the sidelines with Big Momma.

That was my cue. I strolled over to Jimmy, who was still stooped over on the bleacher, looking like he had given up his will to live. "Hi there, Jimmy."

The kid straightened and whirled around. "How do you know my name?"

"I know your friend Ethan."

"Ethan's not my friend. He's a ratturd."

"Well, that's not a very nice thing to say."

"I don't care. Who says I have to be nice?"

This kid was a real winner. I'd best get to the point and quick. "Well, I can understand why you wouldn't be. I heard your lucky lightning bat was missing."

"Do you have it? I can't find it." Jimmy sounded considerably upset.

"What was so special about it? Did it help you hit the ball?"

"No," he said flatly. "I just liked the squiggly mark on it."

"Squiggly mark?" I deciphered that to be the lightning bolt carved on the handle.

"Yeah, but it's gone now."

"When did you last see it?"

"I put it under my bed after practice last night, but when I looked for it this morning, it was gone." He sniffed and scrubbed tears off his fat cheeks.

"I'm sorry. How about I try to find it for you?"

"Will you?" He looked at me with hopeful eyes. I didn't want to deceive him, but I had to find out where he had gotten the bat.

"Yes, of course, but can you just tell me who gave it to you?"

"My brother," he said without any hesitation.

"Where's your brother? Is he here?" I glanced around the field.

"Not anymore. He just dropped me off and left. He plays on the big boys' team."

"Oh, he does? What's his name?"

I held my breath as Jimmy dug his toe into the dirt. And then, in one word, Jimmy confirmed my worst fears.

"Kyle."

I bent over, wincing from a sharp pain in my stomach like I'd been gutted. Kyle had stolen the bat. So, despite everything he'd said to me over the last week, he was a total fake, just as Angelica had said. My toes iced. What else had Kyle lied about?

CHAPTER 27

THE DESIGNATED HITTER

As I looked over to see Big Momma walking off the field, I noticed a man dressed in a suit behind her approaching Coach Bennett. The figure looked visibly agitated as he poked his finger into the coach's chest. Seeing the stranger's spiky sandy hair, I suddenly flashed back to the figure I'd collided with in the locker room just before I had interviewed Coach Bennett. It was him. Could that be Russell's dad? I couldn't hear what he was saying, but I tried to read his lips, and from what I could see, he was saying, "Your time's up."

Patrick ran up to me and grabbed my shoulder. "OK, tell me. What did he say?"

My gaze remained fixed on the interaction. "Do you know the guy the coach is talking to?"

Patrick's eyes followed my gaze. "No, why? Should I?"

"You two ready to go?" Big Momma asked as she caught up to us.

"Oh, yeah, I've been ready." Patrick glanced over his shoulder at Evan. "You ready, Ev?"

I nodded. I was barely paying attention to anything they said as we careened toward the car. I opened the passenger door and poured myself into the seat, feeling like someone was pounding me on the chest. I scanned the car, hearing muddled and garbled voices as if I was stuck in a giant bubble.

Kyle. This entire time, it had been Kyle. Both Angelica and Patrick had been right. So, had Kyle only been pretending to like me this entire time, just using me to find out what I knew about the case to make sure I wasn't close to exposing him? How could I not see it? Had my infatuation with Kyle clouded my judgment?

I'm such an amateur! Every detective in all the shows I watched constantly espoused how you can never get emotionally involved in a case because it always came back to bite you in the end. And I went and did just that.

Now I have to tell Jayden that not only was I blindsided, but also it was his bestie who stole the bat. How was I going to do that?

And I still hadn't figured out why the man from the locker room was yelling at the coach yet again? And what did he mean by the coach's time was up? Patrick grabbed my shoulders from the back seat, and his words finally burst through my befuddlement bubble. "E, for the hundredth time, who is Jimmy's brother?"

I turned around to face him; his vibrant green eyes intensely focused on mine. The pounding in my chest subsided as I took a deep breath.

"We're here," Big Momma announced as she parked the car in her driveway, breaking my trance. "Get inside. It's almost time for my prayer circle."

"Kyle. Jimmy said he got the bat from Kyle," I whispered, still not wanting to believe it as I reached for the door handle. But now, after saying it out loud, it was finally sinking in.

"*Ay, caramba!* Jayden is gonna freak when he finds out," Patrick exclaimed as we burst through the front door into the living room. "I told you. He's always been shady."

Patrick was so excited he bumped into the curio in the foyer, causing Big Momma's crystal figurines to tumble all around.

Big Momma waved her crooked finger at us both. "Alright, you two, be careful. If you break one of my ornaments, I'll have both your hides," she said before closing the front door behind her and placing her keys on the hook beside the door. "I'll put on a pot of coffee." She strolled toward the kitchen. Patrick and I followed, taking seats at the bar in the kitchen.

"So his little brother had the bat this entire time? I do declare, I didn't see that coming, but I'm not at all surprised. I told you I didn't trust him. A leopard never changes its spots." Big Momma set two mugs of coffee in front of us.

"That's what I said," Patrick said, blowing on his coffee before taking a sip.

"Really? Cause, until earlier today . . ." Still feeling the sting of Kyle's lies, I fell silent and swallowed hard. I cleared my throat and tried to regain my composure as I shifted on the barstool. "I can't believe you aren't a little surprised."

"Evan, honey, keep living; after a while, nothing surprises you." She laughed quietly, almost to herself. "So, Mr. Evan, the big question is, whatcha gonna do next?"

Patrick swiveled from side to side on the stool. "Yeah, E, are you gonna confront him?"

"I don't think that's a good idea. We still don't know the exact whereabouts of the bat. It'd be his word against mine. Besides, I'm almost positive he didn't act alone. Coach Bennett has a hand in this as well."

"Coach Bennett?" Patrick almost fell off his stool.

"He had all those casino brochures on his desk. Plus, all those clandestine meetings with the guy in the suit telling him he was running out of time, and he better settle up."

"We know Kyle is involved. Maybe if you confront him, he will rat out the coach."

"That's not a bad idea," I said, pleased Patrick was putting it all together. "But then it would just be Kyle's word against the coach, and you know who they'll believe. I need solid proof."

"Yes, you do," Big Momma said, pointing at me.

"But how are you gonna get it?" Patrick asked.

"I need to catch them both with the smoking gun."

"You mean with the thunder bat," Patrick chuckled.

I appreciated Patrick's humor, but I was deep in thought. "I just need to figure out how to do it."

Big Momma raised her eyebrows. "Well, the best way to catch a mouse is to lure him with cheese because a mouse can never resist a tasty morsel of cheese, no matter how hard it tries."

"A mouse and cheese? How does a mouse wanting cheese . . ." I pictured a mouse delicately trying to acquire cheese off of a mousetrap. In an instant, I understood what Big Momma was saying.

My eyes lit up. "Oh, Big Momma, you're so right. Thank you." I rushed around the bar and gave her a big kiss.

"Ya'll just be careful. Just like animals, people fight for their lives when they're cornered," Big Momma warned.

"We will. Love you." I ran to the front door. "Come on, Pat, we have a lot to do, and you play a big part."

"Um . . . me?" Patrick pointed his thumb back at his chest.

"Yes, *you*. We're working this case together, remember?" I patted him on the back. "Now we have a trap to set."

"Well, you two work on that. I need to get on my prayer circle call." Big Momma walked into the kitchen.

Big Momma was part of her church's prayer circle. They would all call each other on what Big Momma called a "party line" and say prayers for one another. Big Momma said that you could never have too many people praying for you, so she would take as much prayer as she could get.

"So, what exactly do you want me to do?" Patrick asked. I could hear the hesitation in his voice.

"I need you to set the trap for Kyle. How are you at being stone-faced? Think Gibbs on *NCIS*."

"E, I don't know . . ."

"Evan, can you come here?" Big Momma shouted from the kitchen.

"Hold that thought. She can never figure out how to add calls on the phone. I'll be right back," I told Patrick before joining Big Momma in the kitchen.

"I think I figured it out," Big Momma said, punching a button on the phone before placing it back up to her ear. "Sister Johnson, are you there?" She smiled. "OK, great. How about Sister Wesley?" She paused. "No Sister Wesley?" She nodded. "OK, I'll get my grandson to add her because we can't start without her. She told me on Saturday she needed to be on this call; she needs special prayer because her brother is gambling again. From what I understand, it's gotten pretty bad."

Hearing the word "gambling," a switch clicked in my head. The rude guy who collided with me in the locker room said, "you better settle up." Christian said Russell's Dad said, "it better all be here." And the guy at Little League practice said, "your time's up." The threatening guy in all those scenarios was wearing a suit, and now I was certain he was the same person: Russell's Dad.

"Big Momma, is Sister Wesley's first name Jessica?" I said, bouncing up and down.

"Evan, what in Sam Hill has gotten into you?" She put her hand in her hip. "Yes, it is; why?" She sighed. "Are you going to help me get her on the line or not?"

I grinned from ear to ear. "I know exactly who her brother is and why he wants to throw the game."

CHAPTER 28

THE HIT AND RUN

I followed Patrick as he walked over to Big Momma's car and re-trieved his skateboard. I'd already filled him in on everything after I finished setting up Big Momma's prayer circle party line.

When I caught up to him, he abruptly stopped and grabbed my forearm. "I can't believe you just put all of that together. This detec-tive mumbo jumbo suits you."

"I did have some help." I smiled.

He grinned. "Big Momma?"

I laughed. "And someone else." I pointed toward him.

"We are pretty amazing together." He tightened his grip on my arm.

My eyes shot down to the sidewalk as my heart pounded in my ears. "Well, there are still a few lingering details I need to sort out."

I slowly looked up into Patrick's eyes. A strange calm came over me. Despite all my confusion about Kyle, I stared at Patrick, amazed at how despite our friendship waning over the past few years, we were able to pick back up where we left off, without a hitch, to bor-row one of Big Momma's funny sayings.

Patrick gently grabbed my arm as he stood his board next to him and leaned against it.

"Listen, Evan . . . um . . . I've been meaning to tell you for a while now how sorry I am about your mom."

I immediately felt moisture forming in my eyes. I refused to look up, despite Patrick's gaze hot and heavy on me. You would think after a year, just the mention of my mom wouldn't immediately cause me to blubber like a baby. But Big Momma said everyone grieved in their own way and in their own time.

"She was like my second mamá . . . She got me. She understood what it was like being biracial."

I smiled through my tears. Big Daddy was Irish. He died when I was five, but between Mom and Big Momma constantly telling me stories about him, I'd always felt like I knew him too. "Yeah, she really liked you." I looked at Patrick, recognizing how challenging it must be to have a Latin mom and a white dad, especially in Texas.

"I tried to call you a few times after I heard to check on you . . ."

"I know . . . I just wasn't ready to . . ." My voice trailed off as I tried to regain my composure. Patrick had left me tons of messages, but at the time, I hadn't been in a place to talk to anyone.

"I know it's not the same thing, but when my parents first got divorced, my entire world sucked big time, so I can't even imagine what you must be going through."

I smiled, allowing Patrick's words to create a warm pool in my chest. Now I remembered why we were best friends.

"If you ever need . . . or just want to talk. I'm here for you, *amigo*."

I looked up, meeting Patrick's eyes. "Thanks." Patrick still had his hand on my arm. I focused on Patrick's full, pink lips, and my stomach cramped, the same sensation I'd had when I'd been reading the book the night before. My right leg began to tremble as I tried to rebalance onto my left side. I slightly pursed my lips together, placing my tongue on the back of my front teeth. Something drew me toward Patrick. I was elated, but at the same time, I wanted to turn and run away as fast as I could.

My uncertainty slightly diminished when Patrick tilted his head and his lips curled upward as he continued gazing into my eyes. It was as if time stood still as we stood paralyzed in each other's stare. We inched closer to one another. I was terrified, sensing the heat coming from Patrick's body in waves. The intensity became too much, causing me to cast my eyes down toward Patrick's chest, which was now only a few inches from mine. Patrick placed his hand on my chin, guiding my eyes back to meet his. My heart raced, beating so hard I could feel it in my throat. Patrick crept even closer, allowing me to feel short bursts of Patrick's breath hitting my face. We both leaned in, and just as our lips were micrometers from colliding . . . HONK! HONK!

We both jumped out of our skins, toppling over, skateboard and all, as we looked to see a car headed straight for us. Neither of us had realized we were standing in the middle of the street. Patrick, whose hands were still on my shoulders, shoved me back onto the sidewalk, and the momentum caused him to collapse on top of me.

I winced from a sharp pain that I soon realized was caused by my elbow striking the ground. The car screeched to a stop. "Get out of the street, Sissy Sinclair!" someone yelled from the vehicle.

Hearing my infamous alias, my eyes grew wide as I frantically wiggled out from under Patrick. I sat up, catching a glimpse of a male figure on the passenger's side that I couldn't clearly make out other than his long blonde hair. There was a flicker of light from inside the car, and then it sped off.

Standing up, I brushed the grime off my jeans. My breath came fast as I struggled to calm myself down. Patrick jumped up nervously as well, seeing the scrap on the back of my elbow. "Evan, you're bleeding. Are you OK?" He took a step toward me.

I quickly backed up beyond his reach. I flipped my arm to take a look. I hadn't even noticed the cut. Normally, seeing blood would make me woozy, but my mind was on other things, like who was in the car and what exactly did they see?

"I'm fine," I said, keeping my distance. I stared straight ahead. What had just happened? We were almost hit by a car. We had almost . . . kissed? Or was I hallucinating?

"Don't worry about me. I'm fine, and it looks like my board is too," Patrick said, trying to make light of the situation.

I snapped back to reality, noticing Patrick picking his skateboard off the ground and inspecting it for damage. My momentary freak out had made me space out on the fact that if it hadn't been for Patrick pushing me out of the way, we both would've been mowed down. "Oh, Pat . . . " I walked over to him, feeling mortified.

He took a step forward and said, "I'm just messing with you, E."

We both looked at each other for a few seconds before I broke the silence. "I guess I owe you now."

Patrick grinned. "No need to get dramatic but consider us even. Are you sure you don't want to go inside and have Big Momma take a look at your elbow? I speak from experience when I say she does a great job of patching you up."

"No, I'm fine." It amazed me that Patrick was handling the incident so calmly. It finally hit me that this Patrick was far different from the Patrick I'd known in elementary school.

Patrick looked toward the ground. "So . . . about earlier . . . before that car sideswiped us . . . hmm . . ." He looked up at me. "Things got kinda . . ."

"It's cool." The words just flew out of my mouth. I didn't want him to finish that thought. I didn't know what I was more afraid of, what he was going to say or what my reaction would be. "We don't need to talk about it," I said, taking a step back.

Patrick's face fell before he looked down at the street. "OK, so are we good?" He slowly raised his gaze, allowing me to look directly into his earnest, bright green eyes.

I sensed his nervousness, but more than that, his sincerity. It then dawned on me that despite what I'd done to him, Patrick would never deceive me the way Kyle had. The way he had gotten so upset earlier about my run-in with Christian had been the polar opposite of Kyle. Patrick truly cared about my well-being. Other than Big Momma, that was something I hadn't experienced so intensely since Mom had died. The last thing I wanted to do was make him feel bad. I grabbed his arm, pulling him closer. "Yeah, we're good."

Patrick smiled, moving closer and putting his hand on my shoulder.

We both flew backward as a car rapidly pulled up beside us. My heart almost burst out of my chest. I just knew the car from before had come back to finish us off. Or even worse, they just wanted to mock me again. That is until I recognized the make of the car and saw the driver. Dad had a look of confusion on his face. My heart skipped again. Oh God, I hoped he hadn't seen what had just happened between Patrick and me.

"Evan, what are you doing out here? And who's that with you?"

"Dad! You scared the bejesus out of us," I said when I finally caught my breath.

"*Hola*, Mr. Sinclair! It's me, Patrick." Patrick hesitantly waved his hand, still looking shaken.

"Oh, Patrick." Dad gave him a slight smile. "I didn't recognize you. How have you been?"

"Fine, Mr. Sinclair. Thanks for asking." Patrick sounded more confident. "It's getting late. I better be on my way before it gets dark."

Dad noticed Patrick's skateboard. "It's getting dark. Why don't I give you a ride?"

"Oh no, you don't have to . . ." Patrick started to protest.

"I don't want your mom worrying." I'm sure even Dad remembered what a worrywart she was.

"It's only two blocks away. I'll be there in no time." Patrick jumped on his skateboard, flipping it around to face me. "Evan, call me tonight. We can figure out that project." He nodded at me before flipping around further to address Dad. "Nice seeing you again, Mr. Sinclair."

"You too. Take care, Patrick." My dad turned to look at me, his face hardening. "Grab your stuff, so we can go. What did I tell you about coming to Big Momma's while you don't have your phone? We're going to have a serious talk when we get home."

I nodded, knowing that was coming. I then waved after Patrick, but he was already halfway down the street. Wow, he couldn't wait to get away. Or he just wanted to get home before dark. I wouldn't blame him either way.

As I walked up the driveway, I couldn't help but think that he must have been just as confused as I was.

CHAPTER 29

THE SQUEEZE PLAY

After three failed attempts to open my locker, I finally entered the correct combination. I threw my books inside and began looking for my math book. Fortunately, I only had two classes left before I could go home and continue pondering my prickly predicament. My mind raced faster than the cars in the Indy 500.

It didn't help that I could barely hear myself think amidst the earsplitting chatter in the hallway. Everyone was talking about today's pep rally. They were always held on Tuesdays before the games on Wednesdays. However, this one was for the championship game tomorrow, so it needed to be extra peppy, especially given Jayden's losing streak the past few weeks. I reached up to grab my chemistry book from the top shelf of my locker when a finger tapped my shoulder. Inhaling his woody, citrus scent, I instantly knew it was Kyle.

"E, there you are," said the voice behind me.

Startled, I almost dropped my algebra book.

I flipped around to see Kyle smiling and wearing his baseball uniform — gray trimmed in emerald green, the school's colors. It was a tradition that the baseball team members wore their uniforms to the pep rally before the championship game to drum up school spirit. Truth be told, I thought the players just liked strutting around in their duds, getting all the attention.

"Kyle, geez, you scared the life out of me." Big Momma would say that whenever I snuck up on her.

"I'm sorry. I tried calling you a few times last night. You didn't answer," he said, sounding exasperated.

"After the ice-skating fiasco, Dad confiscated my phone," I said blankly.

"Harsh." Kyle clenched my arm, whirling me around to face him. "I think you know why I'm here." I could barely hear him with all the conversations circulating as the hordes made their way down the hallway.

"Do I?" I wasn't going to make it easy. I tried to push past him, but he wouldn't loosen his grip.

"Look, my kid brother told me that he talked to a black kid yesterday at his Little League practice about his missing bat."

I didn't flinch.

"I put two and two together." He moved even closer, allowing me to feel his breath on my neck. "I know it was you, and I know you know I took Thor."

"So, what if I do?"

Kyle clenched his jaw. "I'm just asking that you hear me out. You don't know the whole story."

"I know enough to tell Jayden."

"You don't want to do that."

"Why not?"

"You want to keep hanging with us, don't you?" Kyle released my arm and put his hand on my shoulder. "Don't you want us to all go to the library and hang out again? All you have to do is just not rat me out."

"You stole the bat . . . your best friend's bat. A bat that means everything to him." I pulled away. "No wonder you kept pointing the finger at Christian, Andy, and Lammy for stealing it."

"I should have known you were too clever for your own good." Kyle flashed a mischievous smile.

"You left the threatening note at the park." I was getting angrier and angrier, my voice rising. "You've been lying to me from the very beginning."

"I had to make sure you didn't solve the case before I could get the bat back to Jayden." Kyle gently touched my shoulder, his voice growing softer. "I made a mistake. I've been trying to make it right."

"What or who's stopping you? Coach Bennett?"

Kyle's eyes grew large, his voice back to its stern tone. "You don't know what you're getting into, E. I will fix this. Just let me do it my way." His eyes were like razors digging into my psyche. "You're so

146 · VICTOR D. EVANS

much cooler than everybody thinks you are. I think we could be really good friends."

I looked down at the floor. Just minutes before, I'd been ready to tell Jayden everything, but now I wasn't so sure.

"Hey, are you still reading the book? How far have you gotten?" Kyle was obviously trying to change the subject.

I looked around nervously. "I've been meaning to talk to you about that. I got to the part in the book where the main characters . . . You know . . ."

He nodded. "Oh, I totally know."

The tardy bell sounded. The hallway was relatively clear now, other than a few stragglers scampering to their classrooms. I knew what I wanted to ask next, but I just wasn't sure I was ready for the answer. But here we were relatively alone, just the two of us. If I didn't ask now, when could I? I took a deep breath, and as my dad would say, *man up.* "Is that why you thought I would like the book?" I asked, looking back down at the floor.

"Well, not exactly . . . But I was kind of wondering . . ." He touched my arm. Kyle leaned in and whispered, "Just how much you would like it." His lips brushed up against my ear.

"Once you start hanging out with us, it is something I would like to talk to you more about. You just have to do me this solid."

I took a deep breath. I'd been racking my brain all day, trying to figure out what I should do. Part of me wanted nothing more than to be best buds with Jayden and Kyle, but would I ever be able to look at Jayden without feeling pangs of guilt?

Sensing my hesitation, Kyle put his hand on my shoulder. "E, you're thinking way too hard about this. It's easy. You want to hang with me and my squad, right? I can make that happen. You just have to keep your mouth shut for one more day until after the championships tomorrow. Then I'll explain everything, and Jay will get his precious bat back. No harm, no foul."

I felt like I was in a tug-of-war. Part of me wanted to run and tell Jayden everything, but the other part wanted to keep Kyle as a friend because we might have the same secret. I dropped my eyes. "I don't want to lie to Jayden."

Kyle's smile disappeared as his voice went from warm to cold. "Look, we do things my way, and things work out for both of us. But if you tell Jay . . ." Kyle tightened his grip on my shoulder and leaned in closer. "I can make your life miserable. You think it's bad now; you have no idea. So, think very carefully about what you do next." He stomped down the hallway.

I stood motionless, my heart sinking into my stomach. Now Kyle's true colors were coming out. All those niceties he had showered me with had been a facade. My stomach tightened. Could I even trust him to keep his word? And even if I didn't tell Jayden and Kyle upheld his end of the bargain, I'd always be under his thumb. Was being popular worth that? That was the million-dollar question, and up to a few days ago, I would've known the answer straight away, but now things were totally out of whack, forcing me to reevaluate everything. I was in a pickle, one that tasted way more sour than sweet.

I hurried down the now practically vacant corridor to the computer lab for my media literacy class. I was supposed to be analyzing a website, but instead, I just stared at the screen. I tried to focus on putting together a plan to expose Kyle for the thief he was, but my mind kept flashing back to Patrick, lying on top of me in the middle of the street like a never-ending montage. His bright green eyes, the warmth of his body against mine.

And there it was again, that queasy feeling in the pit of my stomach, excitement, and terror all at the same time. Part of me wanted to make a beeline for Patrick right this second and ask him exactly what was going on between us. That would be scary enough, but his answer could be even more unsettling, and depending on what he said, it could change everything. And deep down, I was starting to realize that I was craving that change.

Although, maybe I was misreading the situation. After all, I'd thought Kyle liked me, but now, it looks like he had only pretended to like me to obstruct my investigation. Patrick and I had been friends, good friends. But was there more? He had been acting very overprotective lately. He'd bulldozed his way onto the case, and he'd kept mentioning how we made a great team.

OMG! Some detective I was. How had I not seen this? Maybe Patrick had been questioning his sexuality, just as I'd been scrutinizing my own. I couldn't help but laugh out loud. How nice it would have been to talk to someone about these feelings, and I'd pushed away the one person I could have confided in and who would have understood. How could I have been so daft? And even if I were ready to accept my being gay, and I wasn't sure that I was, would I really be able to become an untouchable? And did I even still want to be part of that group?

The bell rang, interrupting my scattered thoughts. I hastily gathered my materials and darted out of the room when I heard a familiar voice behind me.

"Hey, Sinclair, you kiss any boys lately?"

I flipped around to see Andy making kissing faces as he whizzed past me down the hallway. Huh? Why in the heck would he ask me that? So much for his being civil. I should have known it wouldn't last. I shrugged it off and turned back around when a few seconds later, I felt a presence beside me.

"Evan, where've you been?" Jayden, also sporting his baseball uniform, ran up beside me, slapping me on the back. "Man, I've been looking for you all day."

"Cool, you found him," Kyle said, following behind him.

My body shuddered upon hearing Kyle's voice, flashing back to our earlier conversation. "Um . . ." My tongue locked.

"Anything? The championship game is tomorrow. Please tell me you know who has it." I saw the desperation on Jayden's face.

Kyle flanked my other side, glaring at me like his eyes were shooting bullets directly into my chest. Many thoughts floated around in my head, but I couldn't focus on a single one. "Um . . . I don't know just yet, but I have a solid lead."

A smug smile emerged on Kyle's face. "Don't worry. E's got everything under control." Kyle pulled out his phone, his fingers speedily gliding across it. He slid his phone back into his pocket, twisting to face me, forcing me to slow down while Jayden continued jotting forward, passing us both. Kyle's face hardened as he said in a low whisper, "Guess who lives near your grandma's house?" A devious grin formed on his face. "You brought this on yourself, and remember, I can do much worse if you don't keep your mouth shut."

My mouth fell open, but before I could respond, he sped forward. "Come on, Jay, we better get to class." He moved to the center of the hallway, forcing passersby to stumble around him.

A chime emanated from Jayden's hand. He looked down at his phone, and his expression rapidly changed from amusement to shock. "Ooh." He looked at me with his mouth gaping open. "Evan, have you seen this? Someone just posted this on the school's SB," he said, turning his phone around and holding it up to my face.

I couldn't believe what I saw. The trolls were at it again. All the air in the hallway was sucked out as I staggered backward into the locker, trying to catch my breath. I took another look at the picture, and sure enough, it was Patrick and me standing on the street in the front of Big Momma's house with our faces only inches apart from one another. The caption underneath read, "Lovebirds."

"What is it?" Kyle lunged forward and grabbed Jayden's hand, twisting it so he could see what was causing all the commotion. "Wowza! Evan, I had no idea," Kyle said, laughing. "I didn't know Mexican skater boys were your type."

"It's not what you think . . ." I spluttered. I wanted to melt and disappear into the floor.

"Leave him alone, Kyle," Jayden suddenly spoke up. "So what if he is? Who cares? It's not our business."

"You're taking up for him, Jay?" Kyle teased. "Are you sure you aren't gay too?"

Jayden frowned and then clapped back. "Why are you making such a big deal out of it? Are you sure you're not?"

I looked at Jayden. Instead of jumping on Kyle's bandwagon, was he standing up for me? It almost sounded like he didn't care if I was gay or not. I might've expected that from Angelica, but not from him.

"Really, Kyle? What is it with you?" I heard Kushaela's voice over the rumble of the crowd. "You don't have anything better to do than spread ridiculous rumors?"

Kyle was about to respond but turned to see Patrick coming down the hallway. "Oh, look, here comes his Latin lover now."

"Shut up, Kyle," Kushaela said before I felt her hand on my shoulder. "Don't let these ignorant imbeciles get to you. You have nothing to be ashamed of."

My vision clouded as she disappeared into the crowd. I couldn't tell whether it was caused by the tears starting to flow down my cheeks or the rage that was now seeping through my veins. Why was Kyle doing this? I wanted to blurt out his secret, telling everyone how he had betrayed his own bestie. It was only fair now that my deepest secret had been exposed.

I opened my mouth to speak, but I noticed the cocky look in Kyle's eyes and the haughty sneer on his face as he stared me down. I froze with humiliation. How the heck had he gotten that photo? My head swirled as if I'd been hit with a sledgehammer in a *Bugs Bunny* cartoon. I flashed back to the long blonde hair I'd seen in the car that had sideswiped Patrick and me, plus Andy's earlier jab about kissing a boy, and then Kyle's comment about someone living near Big Momma's house.

It was Andy. That's why he was teasing me about kissing boys. He must have snapped a picture using his camera phone while he had yelped at me from the car. That was totally his MO. Not to mention, he and Kyle were, as Big Momma would say, thick as thieves.

Since I hadn't been going along with Kyle's scheme, what better way to discredit me than by making me the laughingstock of the entire school? Now, if I did accuse him of taking the bat, no one would believe me. They would just think I was getting back at him for making fun of me. He knew exactly what he was doing.

"Give it a rest, Kyle." Jayden turned back to me. Seeing my distress, he said, "Don't worry about them, Evan. It'll blow over." He patted me on my back. "I gotta get to class but keep me posted on the bat. I'm counting on you." Jayden turned to Kyle. "And you, leave him alone. He needs to focus on Thor, not some stupid picture." He darted down the hall.

"Hey, Jayden, wait up," Kyle called, chasing behind him.

I stood motionless for a few seconds, trying to digest what had just happened. Kyle had threatened to make my life miserable, and he was already making good on it. I blinked back into reality, realizing I needed to get to class. The bell had already rung. I closed my locker and almost yelped when I noticed Patrick standing next to me. In all the confusion, I'd forgotten all about him.

"What was that all about?"

"You don't want to know," I said, throwing my backpack over my shoulder and setting off down the hallway. "I can't talk right now. I'm late for chemistry." I couldn't be sure, but I was almost certain the few remaining stranglers in the hallway were looking down at their phones and then pointing and leering at us.

"E, tell me! What's going on?" Patrick trailed behind me. "I saw you talking to Kyle. Did you tell him we know he took the bat?"

"Shh . . . Keep your voice down." I looked around to see if anyone had heard. "We shouldn't be seen together. Not right now."

"What are you talking about?" Patrick jumped in front of me.

"Someone posted a picture of us from the other night in front of Big Momma's on the school's SB," I whispered to him.

"What?" His jaw dropped.

"Now they think we're *together*." I winced just saying it.

Patrick shrugged. "And? Who cares?"

I couldn't believe my ears. "I do 'cause it's not true," I said much louder than I intended, causing passersby to turn and stare.

Patrick put his hand on my arm. "Would that be so bad?" he said, raising his eyebrows.

"What?" I jerked away from him. Was he going to do this now? In front of everyone? This whole thing was his fault. If I hadn't started hanging out with him again, none of this would be happening. Andy wouldn't have taken that picture, and Kyle wouldn't have been able to use it to shut me up. "Everything's ruined."

Patrick threw his hands in the air. "I hate to break it to you, E, but everybody already knows about you."

"Shut up! I know what I am and what I'm not." Spittle fell around my mouth as I yelled at him, not caring who saw as a few students gathered around us.

"Do you, E? You aren't even real with your friends, so how can you be real with yourself?"

"That's not true." All I could see was red.

"You think I don't understand?" Patrick's voice softened. "I'm a Latin Catholic. My mom is going to flip out when I tell her, but I have to be who I am, and so should you."

I ignored the pang in my heart and stared at the floor.

Patrick's voice rose, changing the subject. "Did you tell Jayden that his BFF took his bat?"

"Shh!" I shook my head and grabbed Patrick's hand, pulling him over just outside the doorway of the chemistry classroom, away from the other students.

"So, when are you gonna tell him?" he asked, slightly lowering his voice.

I rolled my eyes. "It's complicated." A part of me wanted nothing more than to run and tell Jayden that it had been Kyle who had taken Thor, but why would Jayden believe me over his bestie? Like everyone else, he'd think I was only trying to get back at Kyle for the spectacle he had created. Not to mention, I had no solid proof and still no clue where the bat was.

But now, with that picture out on SnapBabble, my reputation was slipping through my fingers like sand in an hourglass. I needed to acquire untouchable status pronto if I wanted to rebuild my social status. But could I expect Kyle to keep his word, especially after what he had just done? Or should I instead reveal the truth to Jayden in the hope he would believe me and still uphold our pact? Complicated was an understatement.

"Complicated?" Patrick's eyes grew wide. "What's complicated about doing the right thing? This is all about Kyle, isn't it?"

The tardy bell rang, prompting me to inch closer to the doorway. "No. . . well, kinda . . ."

A look of realization flooded Patrick's face. "Ooooh, now I get it. You like him. News flash, E, he's not your friend. He's only telling you what you want to hear to keep your mouth shut. I'm your *amigo,* and I always have been." I could see the waterworks forming in his wide jade eyes. "The Evan I knew would never be friends with a thief. So maybe I don't know you after all." He took a few steps back. "Go be with the stuck-up untouchables. Your secret is safe 'cause you'll never have to worry about me hanging out with you ever again." Patrick stormed down the hallway.

CHAPTER 30

THE CALLED GAME

I entered the classroom with all eyes on me, my face blistering. I didn't think it was my imagination hearing whispers all around me as I took my seat next to Angelica at our lab station. At this point, it was anyone's guess why they were ridiculing me now, the picture on SnapBabble or the dustup I had just had with Patrick. It was all fair game.

Angelica leaned toward me but caught Mrs. McCormack's icy gaze and bolted upright in her chair. She tried to cover by glancing up at the clock over the door.

"You're late, Mr. Sinclair. You and Ms. Tyler better get started if you plan to finish before the end of the class," she said while peering at us from under her horn-rimmed glasses, which connected to a chain around her neck. A student across the room shot his hand up in the air, and she shifted her attention to him.

Angelica seized the opportunity. "That was savage. What have you done now?" She shoved her phone onto my leg under the table long enough for me to see that horrid picture. "And what is this all about?"

I sighed. "I don't even know where to begin."

"Start talking, mister."

"Well, first off, I solved the case."

"You did? Who stole the bat?"

"Kyle."

"Are you serious? I should have known. I told you he was a cray-cray mess."

"Coach Bennett is involved too."

"Really? Now that's extra. Have you told Jayden?"

"That's where the picture comes in. That doofus Andy took it and plotted with Kyle to post it."

Angelica snorted. "Of course, he did." Angelica shook her head. "What *is* the deal with that pic? Have you been holding out on me? Are you and Patrick a thing?"

"No!" I said louder than intended, causing Mrs. McCormack to walk in our direction. Angelica moved the beakers around, pretending to organize the workspace.

"We just need to add the potassium iodide to the hydrogen peroxide, and we should be good." I moved a few of the beakers to the other side of the counter.

That seemed to satisfy Mrs. McCormack, who walked back toward her desk at the front of the classroom. Angelica wasted no time getting back to the subject at hand. "You could do a lot worse than Patrick. I think you guys make a cute couple." She beamed.

"We are not a couple," I managed to keep my voice down this time despite the fact she was annoying me to no end. "Kyle's using the pic to ruin my credibility, so I can't tell Jayden what he did."

"Just 'cause you're gay? Who cares? Screw them." Angelica looked into my eyes before I quickly darted them down at the desk. "Oh, yeah. You care." She lowered her voice to a whisper. "I told you, you fancy Kyle." She sounded just like Patrick.

"I do not," I said a bit too quickly and loudly, causing Mrs. McCormack to once again glance in our direction. We both looked down at the burners.

"Yeah, right." Angelica grabbed my arm. "Why would you even want him as a friend? He's a sad, stupid sod, as your TV detectives would say." She put her hand on her hip. "You mean to tell me that you would rather hang out with some guy who's willing to backstab his own best friend than someone who has been by your side for years and is loyal to you even when you treat him like crap?"

"It's not that simple." I looked down at the table, beginning to work on the final reaction assignment.

She gave me her famous neck roll. "Oh, really, then explain it to me."

"Once I get in with the untouchables, everyone will forget about that bloody photo. If I don't get in now, thanks to that pic, I'm doomed to be labeled a gay nerd all through high school."

She put her hand on her chest. "Oh, boo-hoo. How will you ever survive?"

"You don't get it. You've never cared what people think about you. People aren't always calling you names and laughing behind your back."

"Really, Evan! People call me names all the time. Do you really think I don't care what people are saying about me?" Her eyes flashed with hurt. "You think it's easy being a white girl who constantly gets made fun of for talking black?" Her eyes had become glossy. "Especially when I was just being who I am and speaking my truth." Her nostrils flared. Mrs. McCormack looked over toward us with a quizzical face.

"Why do you think I act like I couldn't care less? That's how I deal." Her voice cracked.

My jaw dropped. It was like I was seeing her for the first time. Her face was solid crimson, highlighting her countless freckles. "I didn't even consider all the crap you've had to deal with too." I looked down. "I'm sorry . . . I was too caught up in how they publicly point out all my shortcomings."

"Miss me with that nonsense. There's nothing wrong with you, Evan." Her voice grew calmer. Mrs. McCormack now stood across from us, but she didn't appear as if she wanted to interrupt. "Once you understand that, then you'll realize it's not the untouchables' acceptance that you need. It's your own." Angelica grabbed her stuff and began tossing them into her backpack before she threw it over her shoulder.

I started to protest, but she waved her arm in the air. "Bye, Felicia!"

"Angelica . . . Wait . . ." I called after her, but she walked out of the room without turning back just as the final bell was ringing.

CHAPTER 31

THE SLUMP

My thoughts were like tidal waves crashing around in my head. I hightailed it out of the classroom as swiftly as my legs would carry me. As I grabbed my books from my locker, I saw a few students huddled in corners, whispering and pointing. I wouldn't consider myself a narcissist, but as Big Momma would say, I would bet my bottom dollar they were talking about me and that picture of me pre-lip-locking with Patrick.

I couldn't believe how I had messed everything up. Not only was my association with the untouchables hanging in the balance, but now even my two most loyal friends, Angelica and Patrick, had thrown me over like day-old broccoli. My stomach pinged with pain because, deep down, I knew I had no one to blame but myself.

Part of me wanted to go lick my wounds at Big Momma's, but I already knew her response. She had made it clear from the start that I should have steered away from Jayden and Kyle with her very Southern warning, "Don't let them make a shade tree for you." I still wasn't exactly sure what that meant, but I guessed it was that they were just using me to find the bat. She had also called me a fool for dropping Patrick like a hot potato, so I could only imagine what she would say when she learned both Patrick and Angelica had told me to kick rocks.

With all the confounded jabber ruminating in my brain, I didn't even remember biking home. I ran upstairs to my room. I staggered like I was in a funhouse filled with mirrors, but the reflections were not my own. Instead, they were of Kyle, then of Patrick, then of Jayden, and finally of Angelica before repeating over and over again, and no matter where I looked, there was no escape. The discombobulation was dizzying, causing me to fall onto my bed. I just wanted to lie and wallow in the bed I had made for myself, the bed of stupidity. The most disconcerting thing was I didn't know what to do to rectify this debacle.

I kept thinking back to what Angelica said about how I needed to accept myself before expecting others to accept me. Patrick had said the same thing when he had said I wasn't being real with myself. But how could I accept myself? According to Pastor Franklin's last sermon, I was an abomination.

An abomination? What did that even mean? So, if I liked another guy, I didn't deserve God's love and grace? Surely, he couldn't have meant that. If I just happened to fall in love with another boy, I didn't deserve to be happy, and God was going to turn his back on me? No, that wasn't the God I had been learning about in Sunday school. The one who fed and clothed the poor. That was not the loving and forgiving God I prayed to every Sunday. While I couldn't be certain how anyone else would react, especially Dad, if he ever found out, I was fairly certain God would be the last person to toss me to the curb for loving someone of the same sex. Right now, God was probably the only friend I had left.

I was wiping away the tears rolling down my cheeks when I heard the front door open. There was no way Dad would be home from work this early. That's all I needed. A few seconds later, there was a knock at my door.

"Evan? You in there?" I recognized Dad's voice from the hallway. I slung my backpack off the bed and sat on the edge, praying he would just leave.

"I know you're in there. I can hear you breathing. Can I talk to you for a minute?" He wasn't going anywhere.

Great, what is it now? "Sure, why not?" I was already too defeated to protest.

He walked in, smiling and holding my cell phone. "Guess who's getting his phone back?" he said, then took one look at me, and his jaw stiffened. I must have missed wiping away a few tears.

He dropped the phone on my dresser. "Hey, what's going on, buddy? You okay?" Dad asked softly.

I looked up at him. That was the most concern I'd heard in my dad's voice in a very long time.

"Does this have to do with Karl and Jason and that thunderbolt bat you're looking for?" His eyes were tight and worried, but surprisingly, I didn't sense anger.

"Their names are Kyle and Jayden, and it's his lightning bat. And yes and no." I stared at Dad, taken aback by the concern I saw in his eyes. Maybe he was genuinely interested. We'd hardly talked, really talked, since Mom had died, and now there was so much I wanted and needed to say, but where would I even start? My confusing feelings for Patrick? My complicated relationship with Kyle? My desire to do right by Jayden? How much I wanted to fit in and not feel so alone and confused? Or how my aspirations of becoming an untouchable were hanging in the balance? I grimaced as my headache intensified.

Dad knelt beside me. "Son, I know we have our differences, and we don't always agree on things. But despite that, I hope you know that I love you, and I never want anything bad to happen to you. I'd do anything in my power to help you."

I saw the sincerity in his eyes. After Mom had died, it had often seemed like we were on different sides. I'd forgotten that Dad was on my side.

"I know at times I can be demanding, but that is just because I worry about you. Why do you think I made you do those text check-ins? With my crazy work schedule, it was my way of trying to stay connected to you." He reached down and squeezed my shoulder.

That was all it took. I was dying to confide in someone, and surprisingly, it seemed right for it to be him. "Dad, I just don't know what to do. I solved the case, but it didn't end up like I thought it would. Nothing is ending up like I thought it would. And now everyone hates me." My voice was breaking.

"So, it does have to do with the missing bat?"

I cleared my throat, trying to regain my composure. "Yeah, sort of. I want to do the right thing, but it might mean I don't get what I want. But then again, I'm not sure I even want it anymore. And no matter what I choose, I'm going to end up hurting someone, and that person could be me."

"I see what you mean. That is a tough call. But the bigger question is, if you don't do the right thing, will you be able to look at yourself in the mirror and feel good about your decision?"

I just stared down at the carpet. I knew I wouldn't be able to look at myself if I didn't tell Jayden the truth about Kyle. But I also knew that becoming an untouchable was something I'd dreamed of since elementary school. The way I saw it, I had two choices. I could keep Kyle's secret and trust he would usher me into the untouchables — but given he had stolen his own BFF's bat, there was no way I could be sure he'd keep his word — or I could tell Jayden the truth and pray he believed me and kept his end of our bargain. Or, more likely, he wouldn't believe me and would shun me as well. Then I would be left exactly where I was right now.

"At work, I run into these dilemmas too, and you know what I ask myself?"

I looked up, eyes wide, awaiting the answer.

"Will I be able to sleep at night? If the answer is yes, then I do it, but if not, then I know it goes against who I am, and I don't want that on my conscience."

"But what if you honestly don't know?" I asked.

"In your heart of hearts, you always know. You're just like your mom in that way. I see her in you every day. She would never purposely harm anyone, and if she did, she would go out of her way to make it right. That's why I know you'll make the right decision."

I tried and failed to stifle my tears. "I miss her so much."

Dad put his arm around me. "I do too, buddy, I do too. But you know what? Your mom trusted us to figure out this whole life thing without her. And I know we can do that. No matter what you're going through — even if I don't understand it — I love you, and nothing in the world can change that."

"Nothing?" I asked, wiping the tears streaming down my face. "But what if I'm . . . not like everyone else?"

Dad was quiet for a long moment, chewing on his lip the way he always did when he was thinking hard. Then, he ran a hand over the back of my head and looked right into my eyes. "I've always admired your courage to be who you are, even when it causes you to get unwanted attention. That takes real bravery. In many ways, you're much tougher than I ever was at your age. I will always be here to support you. No matter what."

I collapsed into Dad's arms, finally feeling safe enough to breach the dam of emotion that I'd bottled up for months.

Later that evening, after I'd cried out every single tear I had left in my body, I got into bed and cracked open my book to see how the real gay lovebirds, Mario and Elio, were faring. The trapeze artists' relationship had fully blossomed, and they were planning to run away together and live happily ever after. As much as I was rooting for them, I realized I was just over halfway through the novel, so something must happen to impede this happy ending. My suspicions were confirmed when Mario's father caught the two of them kissing one night after a rehearsal. In an attempt to hide his sexuality, Mario flung Elio away from him when his father burst into the tent, interrupting their canoodling before Mario's dad beat poor Elio to a pulp.

I closed the book, horrified. Mario had been head-over-heels in love with Elio. In fact, it had been Mario who had hatched the plot for them to run off together and live as a couple. What kind of monster could turn on a dime like that and do something so despicable to the person he supposedly loved?

Kyle. He was that kind of monster. Anyone who could take their best friend's most prized possession could do just about anything. What rattled me the most was that I still didn't fully understand why. Jayden appeared to be completely loyal to Kyle and supported him in all his endeavors. Why would Kyle backstab him? A true friend should never be treated with such impertinence.

A sharp pain flooded my head like I'd been hit by my own lightning bat, a humongous one that finally expelled all the ridiculous notions floating around in my head like cobwebs. The rush of it all forced me to throw my head back onto my pillow. *OMG! I'm that monster.* This entire time, I'd wanted to hang with the untouchables, so I would feel normal, like I fit in. But I had already had that — Angelica and Patrick — and I'd taken them both for granted. My heart panged, thinking about how crappy I'd been treating Patrick in particular. This entire time he'd been a true friend, and I'd been a total numbskull. I hadn't wanted to be seen with him and had even been too embarrassed to tell Jayden and Kyle he had been helping me with the case. Dang, I'd been treating him as bad as Kyle was treating me. I cringed, feeling the knots in my stomach. I wouldn't wish that on anyone. I had been so focused on upping my social status and hiding my sexuality that I had lost sight of what really mattered, having people who were in your corner no matter what.

Big Momma had been right all along: a leopard — particularly one named Kyle — didn't change its spots, and true friends — like Angelica and Patrick — were hard to find, so you should appreciate the ones you had. *Why didn't I listen to her?*

I had to make things right. I just had to figure out how.

CHAPTER 32

THE SAVE

I crawled out of bed the next morning, feeling like I'd finally knocked off the two-ton baby elephant that had made its home on my chest. I put on some Kacey Musgraves and got dressed as I sang along to "High Horse." That song was made for Kyle, and it put me in quite a cheery mood. Not only did I have my phone back, but I also knew what I needed to do to resolve my prickly predicament.

Instead of riding my bike to school, I hitched a ride with Dad because I needed to get there early. In Big Momma's words, I had a lot of crow to eat, so I best get started. I knew the person I needed to start with and where she would be.

As soon as Dad dropped me off, I hurried into the library. Mrs. Harlin nodded to me as I barreled through the turnstile and headed to the back of the room. I saw Angelica's bright red hair straight away as she sat with her back to me at one of the back tables. I ran around to the other side of the table and plopped onto the chair in front of her. She looked up as I sat down with a blank stare and then went back to reading the textbook in front of her.

"Please, just give me two minutes," I said, fully aware of the groveling I needed to do.

"What do you want, Evan?" she asked without looking up.

I didn't have much time before school started, and I still had another stop to make, so best get to the point. "I suck."

She looked up and smiled. "Duh? You're just realizing that?"

"I'm sorry I didn't listen to you. I let stupid things cloud my judgment."

"Yeah, like Kyle." She did her classic neck roll.

I raised my eyebrows. "Trust me, that's so canceled."

"Now you're talking with some sense."

My tone turned serious as I looked her straight in the eyes. "I never should have assumed that you have it easy. Now I get it when Big Momma says we all have our crosses to bear."

"Ain't that the truth?"

"Plus, I love the fact that you're blacker than I am." I grinned.

"Whatever, hunty." She flailed her hand in the air. "That's not saying much. Most white people are blacker than you, Mr. Boot Scootin'." We both fell over in laughter.

"So, am I back on your friends' list?" I grabbed her hand.

"For now, but I'm writing your name in pencil because you're kinda sketch."

That's the Angelica I loved. I took a serious tone. "I am so sorry." I squeezed her hand before releasing it.

"I knew you would come to your senses at some point. I was just hoping it would be sooner rather than later," she said, closing her textbook and placing it on the table. "But what I want to know is how are you going to take down that sleaze, Kyle?"

"Funny you should mention that," I said, "because I am going to need your help with that."

"YAAAS! I'm down."

"Perfect! I'll go over the plan with you during chemistry. I need to . . ."

". . . go apologize to Patrick." She tilted her head to the side. It was uncanny how she always knew what I was going to do before I did it. "Yeah, you better bounce. He's outside the caf with the skaters. You're going to need to do more groveling with him than you did me." She smiled.

"Haha, you got jokes," I said as I got up and headed toward the exit.

Just as Angelica had said, I spotted Patrick behind the caf, watching as his skater buds were doing tricks on their boards in the parking area. I only had a little over five minutes before the first bell rang; hopefully, I would have enough time because this apology was going to be much more arduous than Angelica's.

I walked over to Patrick, who just stared at me like I was wearing the bright purple dinosaur costume I had worn one Halloween when we were eight.

When I reached him, he turned to walk away, but I clutched his arm. "Patrick, please! I know I'm the last person you want to see, but I need to tell you something. Please, will you just listen?"

He pivoted back toward me but didn't utter a sound, only barely nodding his head.

I didn't have time to dawdle. "I'm truly sorry, Pat. You've always had my back, and for the second time during our friendship, I took you for granted. I should never have been embarrassed by our friendship for any reason." I looked right into his sparkling green eyes. "I fixated on being an untouchable so I could hide behind them and their popularity. I now realize I was just hiding from myself."

His eyes softened, but he still didn't make a sound. I took that to mean I should continue. "You were right . . . you were right about everything," I stammered.

He raised his eyebrows. "Everything?"

I opened my mouth, but a frog had buried itself inside and made a permanent home. I cleared my throat because I wasn't going to let it stop me. I moved closer to him and whispered, "Yes, everything." I could feel tears emerging again. "I am sorry . . . so sorry." Dang, I thought I had cried them all out last night.

"It's OK." Patrick held my gaze for a few seconds and went to reach for my hand, but the bell rang, causing us both to start.

"Patrick, you coming?" one of his skater friends shouted as he hurled himself into the crowd now forming at the cafeteria door.

"Are you going to tell Jayden?" Patrick asked, taking a few steps backward.

"Yes, I have a plan. I'm calling it 'The Takedown.' You play a big part in it if you're still interested."

"Are you kidding? Let's take the *pendejo* down." Patrick pumped his fist in the air.

"Brilliant! I got my phone back, so I will text you the details."

"Kk." Patrick turned and disappeared into the sea of bodies heading into the cafeteria.

I smiled from ear to ear as I walked around to the other side of the building. Now, I just needed to set my plan into motion by informing Jayden that he would have Thor back before the game that night. My plan had to be perfect because, to believe it, Jayden would need to catch Kyle red-handed.

CHAPTER 33

THE RUNDOWN

I entered the baseball diamond from behind left field. The baseball field was just east of the school and just over three acres. Elevated steel bleachers ran along the right side of the field, just over the foul line. I hurried across the field, over the pitcher's mound toward the bleachers, frequently glancing back over my shoulder to be sure I wasn't seen. According to Jayden, the team always began practice in the weight room, getting a pep talk from Coach Bennett, so I knew I only had about fifteen minutes before they would descend onto the field for warm-ups. They usually practiced for a couple of hours before the game started at 6:00 p.m. I hoped to be gone long before that. It was time to put the plan into motion. Now, if only my stomach would stop doing flip-flops.

The dugout was a little over sixty feet behind home plate. I positioned myself under the bleachers in the far-left corner, almost directly across from home plate. I pulled out my binoculars to ensure I had a perfectly secluded view of the dugout. Right off, I saw Patrick standing in the middle of the dugout. He looked as pale as a ghost. He kept shifting his weight from one leg to the other and scanning the field as if he was looking for someone. Sweat was streaming down from his dark curly hair to his temples. I wanted to go over and say something to reassure him, but that could ruin everything.

I grabbed my backpack and pulled out my handheld video camera, attaching the directional microphone. Luckily, Dad had bought me the video equipment last year when I had had to do a film project in my Media Immersion class. I had to make sure I was close enough to pick up the audio of the entire exchange that was about to take place. I needed it for backup, just in case my initial plan went sideways.

Just as I had gotten everything set up, I saw a figure enter from the left side of the dugout behind Patrick. I peered through the view-finder, but I didn't need to because once I heard his voice, I knew exactly who it was.

"What the heck? What are you doing here, Patrick? Are you the one who sent me the note?" Kyle's eyes got as wide as quarters before growing cold and dark as he clenched his fist and scurried over to Patrick.

I could see that Patrick was startled as he twirled around to face Kyle. However, he did his best to keep his composure. "Kyle . . . Were you expecting someone else?" He smirked. "I think we have something we need to talk about."

"What is this, some kind of setup? Who put you up to this, your little boyfriend, Evan?" Kyle spun toward the exit. "I'm outta here."

Patrick stood tall, his shoulders back and his voice surprisingly calm as he yelled after him. "I think you're gonna hear what I have to say unless you want Jayden, Principal Albert, and the entire school to know what you did."

Kyle kept walking. He was almost out of sight when Patrick yelled, "We have proof you took the bat."

Kyle stopped in his tracks, twisting around. "You have no such thing." He hurtled back toward Patrick. "You think I'm scared of a gay spic, skater-punk like you." He scowled, clenching his fists once again.

Patrick didn't back down. "Give it up, Kyle. You wouldn't be here now if you hadn't had something to do with it."

"I don't know what you're talking about." Kyle flattened his lips. "I got a note from my coach telling me to meet him here, so I came. Nothing suspicious about that."

"Oh? Well, since I wrote the note, I know it mentioned Jayden's bat. So, the question becomes, why would you and the coach be discussing the bat?" Patrick remained in character. Impressed by Patrick's confidence, I couldn't help but smile as I adjusted the audio levels on the camera to make sure it was picking up every word. I quietly pulled out my phone and sent Angelica a text. It was time to put the second part of the plan into action.

"No, the real question is, why shouldn't I beat you down right now?" Kyle stepped toward him, sticking his chest out.

Patrick refused to let Kyle rattle him. "I know you didn't mention any of this to Jayden. Isn't he supposed to be your BFF? He's been going out of his mind looking for 'Thor.'" Patrick used air quotes when he said "Thor" just to rub it in even more.

Kyle stared at Patrick. "You have no idea what you're talking about. This is a waste of my time." He scurried for the exit once again.

"And miss all the fun? Things are just getting interesting," Patrick said with an assurance that I didn't recognize, but I had to admit that I liked this side of Patrick.

Just as Kyle reached the door, he came face to face with Coach Bennett.

"You're just in time, Coach," Patrick said, raising his voice. "We were just talking about Jayden's bat."

"What is going on here?" Coach Bennett pushed past Kyle, racing toward Patrick. "Some red-haired girl told me to rush down here. Something about an emergency." *Good job, Angelica. I knew I could count on her.*

Patrick scrambled to the other side of the dugout. He was following the plan perfectly. He had been able to keep Kyle in the dugout long enough for the coach to see them together. It was time to implement the third and final part of the plan. My fingers sailed across my phone as I frantically sent a text to Big Momma. I stealthily crawled out from under the bleachers and scuttled over to the dugout. *Hang in there, Patrick. It won't be long now. Just another minute.*

"It's nothing, Coach. This greaser doesn't belong down here," Kyle said with a hint of nervousness in his voice.

"Kyle was just telling me about how he stole Thor from Jayden at your request."

The coach gawked at Kyle. "You said what?"

"That's a lie." Kyle lunged toward Patrick, trying to clutch his arm, but Patrick was able to dart sideways, circumventing his grasp. I jumped too, my heart skipping a beat.

"That's not what you said earlier," Patrick said, keeping the pressure on them both. "We were just on our way to Principal Albert's office to tell him everything."

The coach's face went beet red. "Why, you little . . ." He turned to Patrick. "I don't know what he said, but I had nothing to do with stealing that bat. He confessed to taking it, and I've been trying to get him to return it." The coach shuffled from foot to foot. "I should have told someone, but I was hoping he would recognize his mistake and do the right thing."

"You liar," Kyle yelled, his shoulders shaking. "Yeah, I stole the bat, but I wanted to give it back, and you told me not to."

"So why did you do it, Kyle? Was Jayden getting too much attention? Is that what this is all about?" Patrick's voice remained relatively calm, given the situation.

"What would you know about it? I've been in his shadow ever since Little League. He's never had to work hard for anything. Everything just comes naturally to him. I had to practice every day and every night just to keep up. It's not fair." Kyle's face reddened as his voice grew louder. "I just wanted to level the playing field. I found the bat first, and I just happened to put it next to his stuff. Before I knew it, he was using it and getting all the attention. That should have been me!" He took a deep breath and began to calm down slowly. "I was going to give the blasted bat back once he lost a few games. I didn't expect my brother to find it and start using it. That's how Coach found out."

"And what, he started blackmailing you?"

"Yeah. He told me to hide the bat until after the championship. If I didn't, he was gonna tell Jayden what I'd done. That's why I came here. When I got that fake note, I thought he finally wanted me to give it back."

Coach Bennett's veins were almost popping out of his neck. "You infantile . . . You just had to keep your mouth shut for one more day." The coach lurched toward Kyle, who jumped closer to Patrick to avoid his reach.

The coach continued yelling at Kyle, "We had a deal, son, and you just broke it. Good things don't happen to those who go back on their word. You're gonna learn that lesson right here and right now. I'm the coach. You think anyone is going to believe you two knuckleheads over me? I'll say the two of you conspired together to steal the bat, and I just happened to be here to catch you both in the act of returning it."

As if on cue, Patrick said, "Speaking of that, where is this so-called lightning bat? You can't say that if there's no bat."

The coach lunged toward Kyle as if he was going to grab him. "You have the bat. Where is it?"

Kyle bolted to the corner of the dugout and reached down into a small opening covered by numerous baseball plates and pulled up what looked like a bat.

"Here it is . . . I put it here right after I got it back from my brother, so if it was found, it would look like it had just been misplaced."

Coach grabbed for the bat. "Give it to me."

That was my cue. I emerged from my hiding spot and jumped into the dugout. "Actually, I'll take it."

The coach turned toward me, flabbergasted. "What the hell? You . . . I should have known. You nosy little busybody. You just can't seem to mind your own business."

I almost laughed, standing just outside the dugout looking down at the coach. I guess Big Momma wasn't the only one who was a Miss Marple. "I've been told I have that problem. But luckily, I have a recording of this entire conservation, so I'll let the story tell itself," I said, pointing toward the camcorder.

"Is that what you think is gonna happen?" The coach sprang toward me. "You're going to give me that camera."

"That won't be necessary," said a voice behind us. "I think we've heard enough."

We all looked at the back door of the dugout, where we saw Principal Albert and Jayden standing in the doorway with Big Momma in tow.

Perfect timing. I glared at Kyle, whose eyes were shooting daggers in my direction.

"I know I have," Jayden said. He walked over to Kyle, who was still holding the bat, and snatched it out of his hand. Jayden inspected the handle to confirm the lightning bolt, ensuring it was Thor before nodding to me.

"C'mon, Jay . . . It was just a joke." Kyle looked down, his face flushed.

After giving Kyle an icy stare, Jayden turned away. At the door, he abruptly pivoted around, speaking directly to me. "You were right. I would never have believed it if I hadn't seen it for myself. Thanks for getting my bat back, bruh."

"I'm sorry it turned out this way." I looked at Patrick. Nothing was worse than the betrayal of a good friend. I knew that firsthand from both sides.

"Yeah, me too," he mumbled.

"For Christ's sake, Alan, whom are you gonna believe? Surely, you're not gonna take those little punks' word over mine?" The coach looked at the principal in disbelief.

Kyle pointed at me as he spewed his hate. "Especially not the word of a dorky fa—?"

"Excuse me, what were you just about to call my grandson?" Big Momma stepped toward Kyle, stopping him before he could finish. "I should wash your mouth out with soap."

"I can take it from here, Ruth," Principal Albert whispered to Big Momma before stepping between her and Kyle. "She's right. Watch your mouth. I won't tolerate such hateful language, young man," Principal Albert addressed Kyle. "You're in enough trouble as it is."

Big Momma might have stopped Kyle, but I knew what he was going to say, feeling the familiar sting of the word as it sent icy shivers throughout my body.

Kyle ignored them, still staring me down. "You're gay, and everyone knows it. People feel sorry for you. They saw you were hanging with me and Jay, so they cut you a break. But that's over now," Kyle seethed.

I took a deep breath. Normally, threats of rumors and social isolation would have devastated me, but at that moment, I couldn't have cared less about Kyle and what he thought of me. I saw Big Momma's mouth open, so I quickly shook my head. I didn't want her fighting my battles, but what happened next took me by complete surprise.

Jayden looked Kyle square in the eyes. "Speak for yourself. Evan can hang with me anytime he likes. You're the one who is ass out."

"We'll see which friends side with you, you blowhard," Kyle sneered.

"Yeah, I guess we will. I'm starting to see who my real friends are." He poked Kyle in the chest. "I have a game to get ready for. I have a feeling things are gonna turn around for me." He smiled at me, causing me to flinch when he said, "I better see you at the game," before he exited the dugout.

The coach tried to follow behind Jayden, but the principal blocked his path. "Coach Bennett, I think you and I have some issues to discuss, don't you?" He raised his eyebrows.

"I have a game to coach. Besides, I can explain everything. Don't listen to a word that kid says or that recording. He probably has already doctored it up. You can't believe anything he says."

"I don't think the recording is gonna be necessary. It was only a backup in case Jayden and Principal Albert didn't make it in time to hear your colorful rendition of the events," I said with a smirk.

The coach's mouth dropped open, but he didn't say a word. He curled his upper lip.

Seeing the coach's confusion, Big Momma explained, "Evan had me fetch Principal Albert ten minutes ago. We've been listening outside the door the whole time."

The principal nodded his head. "Yep, we heard everything right out of your own mouths."

Evan stepped forward. "Principal Albert, I would ask him why he didn't want Jayden to have the bat so the team would be more likely to lose tonight's game and how that relates to his gambling debts."

Principal Albert raised his eyebrows. "You were going to throw a middle school baseball game to cover your gambling debts?"

The coach's jaw dropped. "How could you even know about that?"

I smiled at Big Momma. "You should never underestimate the power of the prayer circle."

Big Momma readjusted the purse on her shoulder. "I'll say a prayer for your family, especially your sister."

I walked over to Principal Albert. "You should talk to a Mr. Harden. His son, Russell, plays for Western. I think he can shed some light on the coach's financial situation."

The coach rammed his body between Principal Albert and me. "He's a kid. He's making all of this up . . ."

The principal interrupted him. "That's enough, Bennett. Come with me now. You too, Mr. Reynolds," he said, pointing to Kyle.

Coach Bennett continued to plead his case. "C'mon, Alan, we can work this out. I made a few bad choices. I got into some debt, and Harden was helping me out. He just wanted his kid to win the championship. No harm, no foul."

Principal Albert ignored him and turned to Big Momma. "Ruth, I am going to need your statement as a witness."

"I'd be happy to oblige; just give me one second." Big Momma ran over and gave me a quick hug. "I'm so proud of you, and I know your mom would be too." I sank into her arms, sighing with relief and grateful I had finally realized that I'd always been surrounded by people who loved and supported me. Big Momma released me and said, "Text me after the game, and I will pick you up."

Principal Albert marched the coach and Kyle out of the dugout, with Big Momma following behind them.

I turned around to see the person I still had unfinished business with Patrick.

CHAPTER 34

THE BENDER

I noticed that Patrick had been standing there staring as if he was in a trance the entire time. We were the last two left in the dugout, and it was starting to get dark. Behind me, I heard the muffled noises of people starting to arrive for the game, mixed with the team coming out to begin their warm-ups.

"Patrick, you okay?" I grinned. "You had me convinced." I moved directly in front of him. "Listen, Pat; I meant what I said earlier. I wasn't thinking straight." I had to stop and laugh at myself. "Literally. You've always been there for me, and I never meant to take that for granted."

Patrick just stared into my eyes. Still unsure why he hadn't responded, I moved even closer to him. He was usually such an incessant chatterbox that his silence was freaking me out.

"Patrick, what's wr—?"

Patrick stepped forward and raised his hand, palm forward. I froze, my stomach tightening. Patrick brushed up against me, so close our legs were touching, his hand still raised. My nostrils filled with Patrick's familiar scent, causing my toes to tingle. I searched Patrick's face, looking for clues as to why he was acting so strangely. His continued silence only created more uncertainty. My mouth flew open, ready to demand he explain himself, when he gave me a beaming smile that immediately sent sparks down my spine, causing my knees to buckle. Patrick quickly placed his other hand on my shoulder, steadying me. I lifted my hand but found my footing just before I grabbed Patrick's. We both stood there frozen with our hands raised, barely touching. I looked down at the dirt. What if I was making a complete fool of myself? Look how wrong I had been about Kyle. I looked up to see Patrick wink, and without a doubt, I knew I was not misreading the signs this time. I slowly interlocked each of my fingers with Patrick's until I felt Patrick's soft, slightly moist palm against my own. After a few seconds, Patrick gave my hand a tight squeeze. "It took you long enough, *Evancito*."

With our hands still entwined, we stood motionless and smiled at each other. After a few seconds, I pulled Patrick toward the dugout exit. "C'mon, let's go to the game and see if Jayden can hit a dinger with his Thor bat. After all, we worked our butts off to get it back."

Patrick laughed. "Hard pass."

I wasn't going to give up that easily. "C'mon, it could be fun. I haven't been to a baseball game since my mom . . ." His fingers tightened as I looked down at our entangled hands. "Or are you just embarrassed to be seen with me?"

"Never." He smiled. "Kk, let's go."

Twenty minutes later, Patrick and I sat on the bleachers watching the massive crowd all on their feet chanting, "Jay-Thor" over and over in unison. I was not a baseball fan, but I had to admit the fervor of the fans generated contagious energy.

Patrick and I rose to our feet just in time to see Jayden saunter out to home plate, holding Thor over his head like he was lifting a hefty barbell in the air. Jayden pumped his arms up and down, livening up the crowd until he slowly positioned himself over home plate. He did a few swing checks before settling into his stance. Western's pitcher, who couldn't help but be a little intimidated by the spectacle he had just witnessed, prepared for his windup before sending a fastball straight down the middle. Jayden didn't move a muscle. The umpire yelled, "Strike One."

A hush fell over the crowd, but it only lasted for a few seconds before they resumed their frantic "Jay-Thor" chant. The pitcher wasted no time sending a second fastball straight down the middle, receiving the same response from Jayden. It was like he was a statue and couldn't move a muscle. The umpire's words, "Strike Two," filled the air. I hadn't been nervous before, but now I had started to bounce from one foot to the other. Even though I knew the bat itself didn't have any special powers, I'd hoped it would give Jayden the confidence he needed to get out of his slump.

Sensing my uneasiness, Patrick discreetly grabbed my hand and squeezed it tight. Just as he did, the pitcher sent another fastball down the middle, but this time, Jayden didn't hesitate as he swung with such power that the contact between the bat and the ball made a deafening pop, followed by the loud cheers of the crowd. The ball easily flew over sixty feet into the air and cleared the field's back fence. Jayden turned and winked at the crowd before beginning his leisurely strut around the bases, making it crystal clear his mojo was back.

Without realizing it, I was cheering along with everyone around me. I wasn't only cheering for me but Mom as well. I had no doubt her spirit was all around me as I jumped up and down. My exuberance must have surprised Patrick as well because he couldn't stop laughing and pointing at me.

"I think I've seen enough. Are you ready to go?" I asked once Patrick regained his composure.

"I thought you'd never ask." He smirked.

We hightailed it off the baseball field and over to the main entrance of the school. Other than a few stragglers here and there, everyone was back at the field witnessing Jayden's comeback.

"So, how are you going to get home?"

"I'm just going to call my mom. I am sure she's wondering where I am."

"Knowing her, she already has the police out looking for you."

"Hey, shut up. She's just overprotective." He bumped me with his shoulder.

"True that. She has reason to be. You do tend to land face-first on curbs."

We both laughed before our eyes locked once again. Patrick broke the gaze and glanced around to determine if anyone was watching us. I bit my bottom lip, trying to find the right words to tell Patrick how reconnecting with him had changed my entire life in ways I still couldn't fully comprehend.

"Patrick . . ." But before I could finish my thought, Patrick leaned toward me and gently touched his mouth to mine, catching me off guard. But something about the softness of Patrick's lips and his gentleness made me step closer to him and press my mouth more firmly against his. Patrick responded in kind, and as our lips interlocked, we both closed our eyes. After a few seconds, we stood back and gazed at one another before he smiled, grabbed my hand, and we continued walking toward the parking lot.

******

One week later . . .

I sat in the school cafeteria eating lunch, but I was not in my usual secluded spot. And I was not alone. Angelica sat on one side of me, and Patrick sat on the other, next to a few of his skater friends. Jayden sat across from him next to Kushaela and a few of his other jock friends. No, I wasn't at the popular table.

I looked over at the so-called popular table to see Kyle sitting with Andy and the other untouchables who'd chosen his side over Jayden's. For the first time in a long time, I had no desire to eat with them. I was happy exactly where I was and also, most importantly, with myself.

I set my sandwich down on the table and picked up my phone. Holding it up in front of me, I snapped a picture of myself sandwiched between Angelica and Patrick. I was posting it on SnapBabble, and I didn't care who commented.

EPILOGUE

It was a crisp fall day in late October. Patrick and I were sitting out-side on the front porch swing, his hand in mine, when Big Momma came out with a pot of coffee, startling us as she whizzed through the screen door. She laughed and said, "Relax, ya'll about to jump out of your skin." She refilled our cups, and the nutty aroma filled the air. "No judgment here."

I turned to Patrick as Big Momma sailed back into the house. "Speaking of judgment, when do you plan on telling your mom?"

Patrick squinted. "Hmm . . . About the same time you tell your dad."

"That long, huh?" I laughed. "Let's just take it one day at a time."

"That works for me," he said, squeezing my hand tighter.

Just as Patrick uttered his last word, a frantic Molly Henderson leaped onto the porch. "Evan! I have been looking everywhere for you. Your dad told me you were here."

This time, I did jump, almost landing my coffee into Patrick's lap. I set my coffee down and stood up. I'd known Molly since we were in elementary school. She was undoubtedly one of the smartest kids at school.

"Well, you found me." I walked over to meet her at the top of the steps. Her breath heavy, her eyes wide, and her blouse disheveled like she had been running for her life. "What's going on, Molly?"

"Someone stole my tablet. It has all my work on it. Without it, I could lose my standing as our class' 'stellar student.' I need you to get it back."

Patrick and I looked at each other and grinned. The game was afoot . . . once again.

ACKNOWLEDGEMENTS

I couldn't have done this without the support of my friends, colleagues, and family members, who kept pushing me to write even when I didn't think anyone wanted to hear what I had to say. Abundant thanks to the Vashon Writing Group, who read every draft and helped me craft the story I wanted to tell. And a big thank you to my "Sweet Cheeks," who supported me every day every step of the way.

ABOUT THE AUTHOR

Dr. Victor Evans is an educator, journalist, and writer with a passion for telling stories featuring LGBTQ voices that often go unheard. As an educator, his research focuses on LGBTQ images in the media and how these representations affect gay youth as they begin to acknowledge their sexuality. Victor has published numerous journal articles and produced a documentary series entitled, *Curved TV*. His fiction works include short stories in literary journals and three upcoming sci-fi books in the *Fantastic World* series.

As an entertainment journalist for over ten years, Victor wrote, produced, and edited for BET, CNN, MTV, and *Entertainment Weekly*. He is currently an Assistant Professor of Communication at Seattle University, where he teaches journalism and multimedia courses. Prior to Seattle University, Victor taught communication courses at Thiel College, Highline College, and the University of Florida. He received his Bachelor of Journalism from Northwestern University in 1995, his Master of Arts in Dramatic Writing from New York University in 1997, and his Ph.D. in Media Studies from Union Institute and University in 2006.

Victor lives with his fiancé on a farm filled with chickens, goats, ducks, pigs, and a peacock on Vashon Island, located just outside Seattle. He is a member of the Authors Guild.

Please visit him at:
Victordevans.com.
Twitter: @victordevans425
Facebook: Victor Evans
TikTok: @victorevans4253

Made in the USA
Monee, IL
07 February 2022